DANNY ORLIS ON THE VALIANT

&

THE GOSPEL COMES TO FIRST CHURCH

DANNY ORLIS ON THE VALIANT

&

THE GOSPEL COMES TO FIRST CHURCH

BERNARD PALMER

CONTENTS

HOMEWARD BOUND!

anny Orlis leaned back in his seat beside the bus window and ran his fingers through his sandy hair. It was 6 o'clock in the morning and they were jouncing over the desolate stretch of swamp road south of Baudette, Minnesota. In another hour they would be pulling up to the hotel at Warroad.

Tex had planned to fly down to Cedarton for Danny and the twins and take them back to the Angle the morning school was out. But at the last minute, the pilot had a call to fly one of the paper company foremen down to the Twin Cities for emergency treatment after an accident, so Danny and the twins had to go home by bus. Not that it mattered. He would have been happy at the thought of going home even if he had to walk.

Danny closed his eyes. For an instant or two the nightmare of the past few days crowded in around him. He could still see Ken's speedboat racing for the dock, could hear the kids scream as they scattered wildly, could feel the shock of the cold water as he dived in to pull the injured boy to shore. He could still–. Grimly he shook himself to force the whole terrible affair from his mind.

"Young man," the elderly woman sitting beside him said tartly, "do sit still."

He turned to look at her. "I–I'm sorry," he answered.

"I should think you would be." She drew her coat about her and turned a little to stare down the aisle toward the driver.

She was a thin woman with a frayed black coat and scraggly white hair. Her nose was thin and bony, and her long, calloused fingers worked nervously with the latch on her purse. "A body'd think a young man would have more respect of his elders," she complained to herself.

"I'm sorry," Danny repeated. "I didn't mean to bother you. I guess I didn't realize there was anyone sitting beside me."

"Well, you'd ought to by this time," she snorted. "I got on the same place as you did – Cedarton."

Ron looked over at Danny and winked broadly. The older Orlis boy stifled a grin.

They pulled in at Baudette and stopped at the depot for a couple of well-dressed Indians.

"Humph!" Danny's seat companion sniffed significantly as they brushed past her. "Humph!"

Danny leaned forward excitedly and peered out the window. The *Valiant* would be riding at her dock in Warroad now. Bill Marsh and his uncle, James Harmon, would be fueling her engine and loading the freight and fishermen. It had been months since Danny had seen Bill.

They were driving west along the Big Traverse of the Lake of the Woods. It lay just north of them, beyond the line of trees. Now they had only to go through a few small villages and they would be at Warroad. His heart started hammering faster just at the thought of it.

"Young man," his companion said imperatively. "Are you familiar with this part of the country?"

"Yes," Danny answered. "I mean a little."

"Perhaps you could give me some information." Her lips were set in a hard line. "I am told that where I am going, I will have to take a steamer."

"A steamer?" the young woodsman echoed. "There aren't any steamers on the Lake of the Woods."

"I beg your pardon," she snapped, getting out her map. "It says right here, ferry. And the only ferries I've ever seen have been steamers."

"The *Valiant* isn't a steamer," Danny smiled. "She burns gasoline."

Mrs. Eunice Davis, for that was the elderly woman's name, eyed him nervously. "Is it a small boat?" she asked. "Is it safe?"

They had been so busy talking that Danny hadn't noticed they had crossed the Warroad River and had stopped in front of the hotel.

"I'm going out on her too," he said to Mrs. Davis. "Why don't you come with me, and I'll carry your suitcase."

"I'll carry my own suitcase, thank you," she bristled. "I'm much too poor to have anyone steal what few possessions I have."

Everyone else got off the bus while Mrs. Davis got to her feet without moving aside to let Danny pass, pulled off her old coat and put on a beautiful mink coat. "I don't like sitting in my good coat," she explained. "Causes the fur to wear."

Danny got off the bus eagerly and helped Mrs. Davis to the sidewalk. Ron got Roxie's suitcase. For an instant the three of them stood looking about. It was good to be back. It was so good to be back!

There was Bill standing on the cabin roof on the *Valiant* looking toward the bus depot. The other passengers had gone inside. Then Danny saw Bill cast off a line, and he realized what was happening. Bill and the skipper thought they didn't have any passengers for the *Valiant*. They were sailing without them.

"Hey!" Danny shouted, waving his arms and sprinting toward the dock. "Hey, Bill! Bill!"

"Bill!" Ron cried, joining his older brother. "Bill! Wait up!"

"Young man!" Mrs. Davis ordered, hobbling after Danny. "Young man! Wait for me! Wait for me!"

The *Valiant* was out in the river and Captain Harmon was turning to bring her about when Bill spied Danny.

"Hi, Danny!" he cried. "We'll be right back!"

The boat swung back slowly and nosed in against the bumpers. Danny went back to meet Mrs. Davis who was standing beside the railroad tracks panting rapidly.

"I do declare," she grumbled. "I thought you were going to run right off and leave me."

"I wouldn't do a thing like that to you, grandma," he grinned.

"I'm not your grandma," she retorted sharply, "and I'm not anybody's grandma."

Nevertheless, she let him carry her suitcase and leaned on his arm as he helped her down the little hill to the dock.

"It's good to see you, guys!" Bill exclaimed as he swung ashore and helped Mrs. Davis.

"You can say that again," Danny said.

"What about me?" Roxie asked, smiling.

"I'm glad to see you too."

The older Orlis boy went into the little cabin and shook hands with Bill's uncle. The thin faced, gray-haired skipper of the *Valiant* looked even older and frailer than Danny had remembered him. But his eyes were still blue and sparkling and his hand was steady on the wheel.

Mrs. Davis entered the cabin nervously, set down her suitcase, which she had insisted on taking from Danny the minute she set foot in the little packet boat, and without a word changed into her frayed cloth coat.

"Let's go!" Mr. Harmon sang out to Bill.

"Just a moment, captain," Mrs. Davis ordered. "I'm not seated yet."

The skipper looked at her evenly. "We're already ten minutes behind schedule, madam."

Meanwhile, Danny, Ron and Bill loosed the lines and the *Valiant* swung out into the river. For several minutes the two boys stood in the stern of the boat looking at the beautiful homes that lined the river, asking questions and talking excitedly. Finally, Danny was silent for a time.

"Bill," he said at last, "you've been telling me everything that you've been doing during the school year, but you've never once mentioned the church or youth group."

A strange look came over his friend's face.

"How about it?" Danny asked. "Are you still faithfully following Jesus?"

Bill colored slightly. "I guess so," he muttered.

"The past few months I've been wondering a lot," the older Orlis boy went on. "You used to write, asking questions about our youth group's work and the church and tell me about yours, but the past few months you haven't even been answering my questions."

"I know, Danny," Bill replied. "You see, I haven't been going to church and youth group quite as much as I should have the past few months."

"Why not?"

"I don't know exactly," Danny's friend said. "I haven't backslid into my life before Christ or anything like that, but since I started going out with Evelyn I just got out of the habit, that's all."

"Who's Evelyn?" Danny asked. "And what's she got to do with your not going to church and to youth meetings?"

"Her name is Evelyn Brown and she moved to town with her parents mid-semester. She's a great girl! I sure want you to meet her."

"But what's she got to do about keeping you away from services at the church?" Danny persisted.

Bill bit his lip nervously. "She just doesn't put any stock in that kind of stuff. She says we're fanatics and all that. But she's an awfully nice girl, Danny. You'll just think she's great."

"We don't want to forget how wonderful Jesus is, Bill," Danny told him quietly. "Even if she is a nice girl, she must not be a Christian and–."

"Now listen!" his friend flared. "Don't you start to preach at me about not going out with any girl who isn't a Christian. I know what I'm doing!" With that he turned quickly and stormed into the cabin.

Mrs. Davis and the twins were the only other passengers aboard on that particular trip. The *Valiant* was out of shelter of the river by this time and was angling into the stiff swells that were running across the Big Traverse. As the little boat bucked over them, one after another, with stubborn tenacity, Mrs. Davis clenched her teeth more tightly than ever. She clutched the arms of her chair with a deathlike grasp.

"C-c-captain," she stammered, her voice quavering, "tell me, is this little boat safe? Is it still seaworthy?"

The skipper turned around and nodded solemnly. It wasn't the first time he had had to reassure an uneasy passenger.

"Absolutely. The *Valiant* is one of the safest boats afloat."

Danny noticed that his old friend at the wheel of the *Valiant* was trembling. His face was gray, and his lips were turning blue. The Orlis boy got to his feet quickly and went up to him.

"Would you like to have me take the wheel for a while, skipper?" he asked.

He thought that he had spoken softly, but Mrs. Davis straightened quickly and stared hard at him.

"He most certainly doesn't want you to take the wheel, young man," she announced firmly. "Do you, captain? Not with the boat tossing around like this."

Roxie came up beside Danny and her twin brother, and Bill approached from the other side.

"Are you all right, Uncle Jim?" Bill asked. His voice was thick with concern. "Are you sure that you're all right?"

The captain clutched the wheel tightly to brace himself and wiped at his moist forehead with a gnarled, trembling hand.

"I don't know what's come over me all of a sudden,"

he said weakly. "I felt all right when we came out, but now I'm shaking inside."

"I know exactly how you feel, captain," Mrs. Davis put in primly. "I feel exactly the same way. And I'm afraid that I'll feel that way until you get this–this little boat back to shore."

She continued to talk, but nobody was paying any attention to her. Mr. Harmon stiffened. His body began to tremble. Then slowly his knees began to buckle, and he sank to the floor.

"Skipper!" Danny cried.

"Uncle Jim!" Bill exclaimed.

Together the boys eased him to the deck, where he lay very still. Ron and Roxie crowded close about them.

THE SICK SKIPPER

Danny Orlis and Bill Marsh bent over the elderly captain who was lying on the deck in front of the row of cabin seats. Roxie knelt beside him and quickly loosened his collar. The color had drained from his face and his thin lips were blue.

"Is he going to be all right?" Ron asked softly.

Danny grasped the skipper's brown, leathery wrist and felt for his pulse. It was faint, erratic, and very fast. His eyes were closed, and his breath was coming in short, uncertain strokes.

"Uncle Jim," Bill exclaimed tensely, "what's wrong? What's the matter?"

The skipper opened his eyes and his lips parted as though to speak. Then he closed them again reluctantly.

The *Valiant* had swung about with no one at the helm. She wallowed drunkenly in the trough of a big swell. The sea rolled under her, and she drifted up to the crest, riding sideways. Then, without warning, she dropped sickeningly into the trough behind it. A cascade of water poured over the rails and foredeck. The boat lurched under the force of it.

Mrs. Davis screamed.

"Young man! Young man! Steer this thing or we'll all be drowned!"

But Danny and the others did not even hear her.

"Bill," he said softly, "I think we'd better turn back. We've got to get your uncle to a doctor just as fast as we can."

The skipper, hearing what he said, opened his eyes and shook his head. "No," he told them feebly, "don't go back. I'll be all right."

"But, Uncle Jim," Bill protested, "you've got to get to a doctor. You ought to have some medicine right away."

"I'll be all right, Billy, "the old man repeated. "Just get me that little pill bottle in my jacket pocket. That's all I need." It was an exertion for him even to speak. "I've got some medicine in there for spells like this. It isn't anything to worry about."

Bill hurried to get the pills from his uncle's jacket. It was hanging on a nail at the back of the cabin. The *Valiant* lurched violently once more and Mrs. Davis screamed again. Her face was pale and drawn and her mouth was trembling nervously.

"You've got to do something, young man," she

said gasping. "Don't just stand there and let this boat upset. You've got to do something."

He took the wheel. Carefully he felt the rudder.

"Don't worry, Mrs. Davis," he told her, trying to sound as calm and collected as he knew he should. "We aren't in any trouble, and we're not going to be."

"M-maybe you're not, young man," she said, her voice tremoring, "but I've had all the boat rides I'll ever want. I'm through with boat rides, and that's for sure. I'll walk before I ever ride on another boat."

Danny Orlis cast a quick sidelong glance down at the skipper and his friend. Bill had just given his uncle the pill and was spreading a blanket over him. Roxie tucked it in.

"Is he going to be all right?" she asked.

"I think so," Danny said. But what if that medicine didn't help the way Uncle Jim had said it would? What should they do?

His heart was hammering against his ribs, and his hands were quivering on the helm of the little packet boat. He brought the *Valiant* slowly about until her blunt nose was quartering into the waves, and she was lifting and falling rhythmically as each new roller broke under her.

Danny heard Mrs. Davis sigh deeply. He gripped the wheel tightly and glanced back. She had relaxed her almost hysterical grip on the seat and was staring down at the skipper.

"The poor man," she said softly. "The poor, poor man."

By this time Mr. Harmon stirred a little.

"Now you'd better lay still, Uncle Jim," Bill said quickly. "Everything's all right. Danny's steering the boat and everything's going fine."

"I'll be all right in a few minutes, Billy," the elderly skipper said. "I'll be all right."

"We're almost to Oak Island," Danny said after a few minutes. "Do you think we ought to put in there?"

The skipper shook his head. "If this lady doesn't get off at Oak, let's go on down to the Angle. I'm feeling a little better now."

"I don't know where I get off," Mrs. Davis put in. "I'm going up in this wilderness somewhere to visit my brother and his family, Winston Douglass. All the information I got was to take the ferry boat."

Danny Orlis pursed his lips.

"I don't remember anybody by that name," Ron said. "Who are they, Bill?"

"They moved in about three or four months ago," the Marsh boy said. "They bought that vacant place up the creek from your place."

By the time they passed Penasse at American Point, the color had come back to the skipper's face. He was sitting on the deck with the blanket drawn up around his knees. His breathing was still short and labored, but there was no doubt that he was feeling better. However, Bill needed to be reassured.

"How're you feeling, Uncle Jim?" he asked for the fourth or fifth time.

The captain nodded.

"Better, Bill," he said. "I feel a lot better now. I knew that I'd be all right as soon as I took one of those pills. They always work for me."

They were along Little McCoy Island now. Danny, who was still at the helm, looked over at the mouth of Pine Creek and grinned widely. There were his parents standing on the dock waiting for them.

"Look!" Roxie exclaimed excitedly. "There's Mom and Dad!"

"And there's the *Scappoose* tied to the dock," Ron added. "Oh, boy!"

Suddenly Danny couldn't get home fast enough.

* * *

The skipper protested loudly that he was all right, but Mrs. Orlis insisted that he go into the house and lie down while the Orlis brothers and Bill unloaded the freight that the *Valiant* had brought up to the Angle.

"Now the boys'll take care of everything, skipper," Carl Orlis put in. "Go in and lie down as Mary says. You've got to take care of yourself."

"Sure," Danny said, "we'll take care of the *Valiant*. You don't have to worry about a thing."

As soon as Bill was sure that his uncle was all right, he went with Ron and Danny out to the *Valiant*. Roxie joined them, helping unload what she could.

"It sure is great to be back," Ron said, taking a deep

breath and looking out across the creek. "Those old fish are just laying out there waiting for me."

"I thought it was baseball that you've got to catch up on," Danny told him.

"I can't neglect those fish either," Ron said. "I'd like to be about four guys for a couple of months. Then I could do all the things up here that I'd like to do."

"Right now, all I can think about is Uncle Jim," Bill said. "I didn't even know that he'd been sick and had seen a doctor. I don't think he's ever said anything to anyone about it."

"I was so scared when he got sick," Roxie said.

They were talking as they walked out on the wide dock. When they reached the *Valiant* again, Mrs. Davis was still sitting there, staring straight ahead. Her fur coat was lying in her lap.

"Oh, Bill!" Danny exclaimed. "We forgot all about Mrs. Davis!"

"Will she be mad!"

They clambered into the boat and entered the cabin.

"Well," the old lady snorted belligerently, "I'm surprised that you came back at all. Is this the way a passenger is to be treated? A good, cash-paying passenger?"

"I–I'm sorry," Bill explained, "but we got so busy with Uncle Jim that we forgot all about you."

"Never mind that. Just start this contraption and take me up to my brother's."

"I'm sorry," he explained, "but this is as far as we can go."

"Isn't your brother coming after you?" Danny asked.

"How could he come after me?" she demanded. "He doesn't even know that I'm arriving today." She laid her coat on the seat beside her and fixed her glassy stare on him. "It's obvious that I can't sit here. You'll just have to take me up to his place."

Bill shook his head.

"I wish we could," he told her, "but we can't run the *Valiant* up there. We can't get past those old bridge posts. And even if we could, the water's too shallow in a lot of places."

Mrs. Davis drew herself up regally. "What do you expect me to do?" she demanded. "Walk?"

"I'll take you," Danny told her, "if you'll ride in the *Scappoose*."

She eyed him strangely. "In the–the what, young man?"

"The *Scappoose*," Danny repeated, grinning at the strange look that came over her face. "That's my little boat. The one tied to the dock."

"Humph," she grunted curtly. "I thought you were trying to get smart with me." She got up stiffly. "If I must ride in the–the *Scappoose* to get there, I'll have to ride in the *Scappoose*." She limped painfully toward the door. "I must *get* to my brother's. Bring my bag."

It wasn't a request but a command.

Danny picked up her suitcase and followed her while Bill pushed ahead and helped her climb out of the *Valiant* and up on the dock.

"Can we go along?" Roxie asked her brother.

"I don't know, Roxie," he said. "I'd like to take you, but the *Scappoose* is going to be loaded awfully heavy."

"But you're just going up the creek," she said. "There won't be any waves up there. Besides, it'll give Ron and me a chance to get acquainted with the Douglass kids."

"I suppose there's a nice-looking boy up there that you'd like to meet."

"There's a boy up there," Roxie admitted, coloring, "but that's not why we want to go. Mom and Dad said that Peter and Ellen Douglass haven't been to Sunday school since their parents moved up here. I thought maybe we could meet them so we could ask them to Bible Club when we get one started."

Danny was interested immediately. "Are you planning on starting a Bible Club at the Angle this summer?" he asked.

"That's what we've been talking about," Ron told him. "We had so much fun in Bible Club back at Cedarton last winter that we thought it would be nice to have something here for the summer."

"And," Roxie added, "we figured there might be a chance of telling some of the kids about Jesus."

"That does sound interesting. I think it would be all right if you ride along. Bill's going to stay here with his uncle and, as you say, there's not much danger that the creek is going to get very rough."

Mrs. Davis wrinkled her nose distastefully as the twins got into the *Scappoose* and sat down, but she said nothing.

Although Danny had only revved up the motor to half speed, the creek was narrow and the trees seemed to be flying past. Mrs. Davis cautiously reached out her hands and grasped the boat tightly on either side with gnarled fingers.

"Children!" she snapped after a moment or two. "Children, leave the young man alone! Let him pay attention to his job. He might put this boat up a tree any minute."

Roxie Orlis's sensitive face clouded and Ron scowled. "Children," he snorted inwardly. But Danny grinned at them and winked.

When they reached the Douglass home the family came down to the dock and helped Mrs. Davis out of the *Scappoose*. For a couple of minutes everybody was talking and laughing at once.

Finally, when they quieted a little, Roxie grasped Ellen by the arm. "I suppose you're Ellen," she said. "Mother was telling me all about you."

"You're Roxie! I've been waiting and waiting for you to get home from school."

"I talked Danny into letting us come along," the Orlis girl said, "so that Ron and I could meet you and your brother. We're planning on starting a Bible Club in a week or two. And we'd sure like to have you and Pete come."

"It sounds like fun," Ellen said. "I've never been to anything like that, but it sounds nice."

"Oh, it will be!" Roxie told her. "We'll have a great time."

The Douglass youngsters were at least two years younger than the Orlis twins. They turned to their parents. "Can we go to the Bible Club, Dad?" Pete asked.

Mrs. Davis glared at her niece and nephew.

"You must not be very glad to see your old aunt," she said, "or you wouldn't be thinking about going somewhere before I even get my things in the house."

"I'm sorry, Aunt Eunice," Ellen explained. "We were just talking about the Bible Club that the Orlises are going to start."

"Bible Club?" the old lady echoed. She turned slowly to her brother. "Winston Douglass," she exclaimed deliberately, "do you permit your children to take part in something like that? Are you going to let them make themselves ridiculous by going to a Bible Club?"

Winston Douglass flushed scarlet.

"No, I'm not!" he exclaimed. "And I'm going to put an end to it right now. Pete and Ellen can't go to any Bible Club. I don't care where it's held. You two, get back into your boat and beat it! Leave them alone!"

"But–" Ron started to protest.

Danny, however, took him by the arm. "Come on," he said softly. "We don't want to argue."

With that he and the twins turned and started back to the *Scappoose*.

"Just a minute, young man," Mrs. Davis called out.

He turned and went back to her.

"Here!" She dropped a ten dollar bill into his hand. "This is for bringing me up here."

Danny shook his head in protest.

"I don't want anything for doing that," he said, handing the money back to her. "We don't charge for being neighbors and friends here on the Angle. We've all got to help each other. But thanks anyway."

Again that odd, perplexed look crossed her face momentarily.

When the *Scappoose* was out in the creek and they had rounded the bend on the way home Roxie said, "Oh, Danny, I–I don't know what to do! Ever since Mom and Dad wrote us about Ellen and Pete we've been praying that we could help bring them to Christ. Now we can't even go up there and visit them, let alone talk with them about the Lord or invite them to Bible Club or to Sunday school."

"But," Ron put in with firm determination, "we can still pray for them. And that's the most important thing. Nobody can stop us from doing that."

When they pulled up to the dock Bill was there to meet them. Danny could see by his face that something was wrong.

"How's the skipper?" he asked.

"I don't think he's any worse than he has been," Bill answered, "but he had another spell a little while ago."

Danny whistled. "That is too bad."

"I was talking with your dad just now. He's sure that the doctor won't let Uncle Jim keep the Valiant going. And, Danny, he's got to. He's just got to! He and my aunt won't be able to get along unless the Valiant keeps running."

CHAPTER 3

"I'VE GOT TO KEEP GOING!"

For a moment or two the boys stood together on the dock. They were staring silently out across Angle Bay. From somewhere across Pine Creek an owl stirred in a treetop and called out mournfully that dusk had come and that he was about to be off on his nightly search for food. A smile flickered on Danny's lips at the sound. This was one of those things that he had thought so much about when he was in Cedarton. How often he had gone to sleep to dream of the haunting, familiar sounds of the Angle! Dreams that brought a rush of homesickness!

Then Danny saw the shadow that clouded his friend's face, saw the quick concern that smoldered in his eyes. He turned to the twins who were still sitting in the *Scappoose*.

"Ron," he said softly, "why don't you and Roxie go up to the house and see if you can help Mom with supper? Bill and I have some things to talk about."

His younger brother started to protest, but Roxie climbed obediently out of the boat and started toward the house.

"Come on, Ron!" she said. "I want to talk with Mom and Dad anyway. It's been so awfully long since we've seen them."

When they were gone Danny turned once more to his companion. "You're awfully worried about your uncle, aren't you?" he asked.

Bill Marsh nodded.

"I guess it was such a shock to me. I didn't know until today that he'd even been sick."

They left the dock together and went down along the creek to one of the guest cabins. "Was this last spell any worse than the one he had on the boat?" Danny asked after a time.

"Uncle Jim didn't think that it was bad at all, but it scares me, Danny. I just can't help it."

There was a long silence.

"You know what we used to do when we got in a tight spot, don't you, Bill?" he asked at last.

"I have been praying, Danny," his friend answered miserably. "I've been praying ever since Uncle Jim got sick today, but I can't see any difference in him."

The Orlis boy laid his hand on his friend's arm.

"Why don't we go in here where we can be alone," he asked softly, "and pray together?"

Bill Marsh did not answer. He allowed himself to be led into the little cabin where he knelt with Danny beside the bunk. The Orlis boy prayed first and Bill followed. He prayed a short, halting prayer, asking God to help his uncle get well.

There was nothing wrong with what he said, and he sounded serious enough, but somehow his praying bothered Danny. Not that the stumbling or the lack of words meant anything. Rather it was the way Bill prayed, as though he were woodenly repeating something he thought he should say. It was not as though he believed that God was really listening, waiting to answer him.

When Bill got to his feet the same look of concern lingered in his eyes. The same fear was written on his face.

* * *

The following morning Carl Orlis came into Danny's bedroom shortly after daylight and awakened him.

"Danny!" he said, shaking his son vigorously. "Danny, there's something I want you to do. Come on. Get up."

The Orlis boy shook himself to brush away the sleep that still half-drugged him.

"What's the matter, Dad?" he asked.

"I think you'd better go on the *Valiant* with Bill today," Carl Orlis told him. "Mom and I talked it over. We're afraid that Uncle Jim isn't able."

Danny swung his feet over the side of the bed and reached for his jeans.

"Ron and I were going fishing today," he said, "but that can wait. This is more important."

"Yes," Mr. Orlis said, "this is a great deal more important."

Down in the kitchen Jim Harmon protested vigorously.

"Now, Carl," he said, "this is all a lot of foolishness for you to send Danny along with Bill and me. I've had these spells before, and I always get over them. I feel as well now as I ever have."

"You look a little shaky to me, Jim," Carl said.

"But I'll be all right. Besides, Danny's been gone from home for quite a spell. You let him stay here and enjoy himself. He's not anxious to go traipsing back to Warroad."

"He'll have plenty of time to be at home this summer," Carl Orlis said, looping his arm about his old friend's shoulder. "Now you just sit back and give the boys orders. Let them do the work. They can take care of everything."

"But I don't need anyone to go along and help, Carl," the elderly skipper protested. "I can manage."

Nevertheless, he was panting heavily by the time they reached the *Valiant* and Carl Orlis helped him get aboard and down into the cabin.

Bill and Danny started the engine and got the fish boxes aboard. Exactly on schedule at 6:30 in the morning they backed the *Valiant* away from the Orlis dock and headed up the creek toward open water.

"If it weren't for the worry of having your uncle sick, we'd have a lot of fun on this trip." Danny said under his breath to Bill as they stood close together at the helm, "It's something to be handling the *Valiant*, isn't it?"

Bill nodded.

His uncle sank heavily into one of the front chairs in the cabin and was sitting with his eyes closed. Only the sallow color in his cheeks and the dark, haggard look about his eyes betrayed that he was ill.

"He's going to be all right," Bill said softly to Danny Orlis. "Isn't he, Danny? Don't you think that he'll get over this?"

"We'll have to put our trust in the Lord to heal him," the Orlis boy answered.

The big lake was glassy calm, and they made good time even though they had to make the run up to Northern Lights' Musky Camp to pick up a couple of fishermen and stop at Flag Island for a diesel motor that needed repairing. The skipper sat up for most of the trip, but while they were stopped at Flag he crawled down into the prow of the boat and stretched out on the bunk to rest. Bill stopped working two or three times and went inside to see how his uncle was doing.

"I'm all right," he said at last. "Don't worry about me, and get this boat loaded so we can go on to Warroad."

Finally they had the motor aboard and began to plow across the Big Traverse. They pulled into the Warroad River just as the noon whistle sounded.

The skipper pulled out his watch and looked at it.

"Not bad," he said approvingly. "You boys took all that extra time to load at Flag Island, and we're still only thirty minutes late. That's not bad at all."

Danny eased the *Valiant* expertly up to her berth just above the Fisheries, and Bill threw out a line and snubbed her tightly against the bank.

"Go and sit down, Mr. Harmon," the Orlis boy told him as the elderly skipper moved slowly back to the pile of fishing gear and freight in the stern of the *Valiant*. "I'll unload this stuff while Bill goes home after the car."

"I don't need a ride home," the skipper grumbled good-naturedly. "I've never seen the day when I couldn't walk up the street to our place."

"Just the same, we're going to see that you get a ride today."

Bill's dad came back with him in the car and insisted that Mr. Harmon go to the doctor.

"But I'm all right," he protested almost angrily. "Just leave me alone and quit worrying about me. I'm all right."

"And," Bill's dad replied, "we want to see that you stay that way." He got into the car and the skipper went around to the other side and opened the door.

With his hand on the door handle he stopped and turned to Danny and Bill. "You guys will take care of everything down here, won't you?" he asked.

They both nodded.

"Dad must figure that Uncle Jim's awfully bad

or he wouldn't be taking him to a doctor." Bill said when the car passed from view.

Danny Orlis did not answer.

The boys unloaded the *Valiant* and took her upriver to the gas pump where they filled her big tanks. Then Bill got out the grocery lists that people on the Angle had given him. There was always shopping to do after every trip.

"Now," he said, "we'll go and buy the things we have to get for the Nelsons and the Douglasses and for your parents, Danny. Then we'll be all set for tomorrow."

Back at the dock they tied the *Valiant* securely to her mooring posts and made their way across the tracks to the business district of town.

"There's Dad's car in front of the doctor's office," Bill said, concern edging his voice. "The doctor must still be working with Uncle Jim."

"We've got to trust, Bill," Danny repeated. "God tells us that we should pray for help and guidance in the things that we need. And then we must put our trust in Him to work things out in accord with His will."

"I know all that," Bill replied, his voice rising, "but why would this have to happen to a nice guy like Uncle Jim? He's gone to church all his life and has helped with Sunday school and missions and everything. Why should someone like him have to get sick?"

"I don't know the answer to that one," Danny replied, "and I don't know whether anyone else does. But Dad always says that God has never promised to tell us why things happen the way they do. And He has never said that a follower of His will have life any easier because he's a Christian. He says that sometimes it's harder. All He promises is that He will take care of us and supply our needs, if we call on Him."

"I guess you're right," his friend said. "I've heard that often enough and know Bible verses to prove it. But it's sure hard to understand why Uncle Jim would have so much trouble."

The Orlis boy said nothing. That sort of thing had bothered him a lot too.

By this time they reached the shop. "Let's go in here for a minute," Bill said. "There's somebody in here that I want to see."

They went into the shop and Bill stopped beside the magazine rack. A tall, slender brunette, with flashing dark eyes and lips that were much too red, walked up to them.

"Hi, Bill," she said, smiling. "I was wondering when you'd come to see me. I saw the *Valiant* come in a little while ago."

"We had some errands to run," he told her. Then he remembered Danny and introduced him to her. "This is Evelyn. You know. I've told you about her." They talked for a few minutes.

"Hey," Bill said at last, "if you don't have to work tonight, why don't you get a girl for Danny, and we'll all go out somewhere?"

"That sounds like fun," she replied. "Could you take the *Valiant*?"

"Maybe! I'll talk to Uncle Jim. We'll see you tonight about eight."

She smiled and winked at him.

When they were outside once more Bill turned to Danny Orlis.

"Well," he said, "I guess I fixed that up for you."

"I guess you did," Danny retorted irritably. "Why didn't you let me pick my own girl? I know a bunch of kids here in town."

Bill colored a little.

"To tell you the truth, Danny," he said, "Evelyn thinks that most of the girls you know and would be apt to date are old-fashioned and boring."

"Maybe she'll think I'm old-fashioned too," the Orlis boy replied.

They finished their shopping in a few minutes and stopped by Jim Harmon's to see how he was. The elderly skipper was sitting on the side of the bed and Bill's aunt was standing beside him.

"Three months!" the skipper was exclaiming. "We're just going into the season, Carrie. How can I lay off for three months?"

"You know that the doctor said you must rest that long, James," his wife countered. "You'll have to do it."

His forehead wrinkled.

"I know what Doc said, Carrie," he said softly, "but we borrowed on the *Valiant* to get that new motor this spring. We've got to keep her running in order to pay off the note. I know I ought to quit, but I can't. I've got to keep going!"

CHAPTER 4

A DOUBLE DATE

Danny Orlis and Bill Marsh stood awkwardly in the skipper's living room. The boys hadn't intended to eavesdrop. Bill had knocked lightly on the door, as he always did to let his aunt know that he was there, and they stepped inside. But neither she nor her husband heard them.

"But you heard what the doctor said," his aunt continued. "You know that a spell like you had is a warning for you to rest and be extra careful. Couldn't Billy keep the *Valiant* going?"

"I thought about that," the skipper replied. "He knows all the channels and the people on the islands, and the people at the Angle like him. If he had a good, reliable man to help him, I'm sure that he'd get along fine."

"Well, then, it's all settled. We'll hire someone to go on the *Valiant* in your place, and you can rest. There's nothing for you to worry about."

"It's not as easy as all that," he said. "Don't you remember how much trouble I had getting good help before Billy got old enough to go with me? It won't be any easier now. And besides, if we should find someone who is good, we'll have to pay him so much that we can't get by." The elderly skipper shook his head. "No, Mother," he said weakly, "I don't know just what we'll do."

"Now, James," she said calmly, "the Lord will look after us. We don't need to fret."

Mr. Harmon smiled and patted her arm tenderly.

"I know that you're right, Carrie," he told her. "I shouldn't be doubting the Lord."

"We'll just talk to Him about it," she said in that same matter-of-fact tone. "The Bible tells us that's what we ought to do with our burdens instead of trying to carry them ourselves."

Slowly the old couple got to their knees beside the bed and began to pray. Danny had never heard prayers like those before. They prayed so earnestly, with such assurance, that one would have thought the Lord was actually in the room listening to them.

Indeed, it seemed to Danny that He must be. Suddenly it seemed almost a sacrilege for them to stand there listening. Danny touched Bill on the arm and motioned significantly toward the door. They turned quietly and tiptoed back outside.

They were silent for two or three minutes as they walked across the street toward town.

Finally Bill said, "What do you think, Danny?"

The Orlis boy shook his head. "I don't know," he said. "I sure feel sorry for your aunt and uncle. They've got a real problem."

"I don't know whether I could manage the *Valiant* without somebody along who knew exactly what to do," his friend said. "It's a big job. Do you suppose you could help me, Danny?"

"I don't know whether I can or not," Danny Orlis repeated. "But I sure would like it. It'd be fun going into Warroad one day and back out the next, hauling fishermen and freight."

"I'll say. Especially if you were along, Danny. It sure has been lonesome around here without you. We could sort of make up for lost time."

The Orlis boy was silent. Bill Marsh was just about the best friend that he had. It would be fun spending the summer on the *Valiant*, working with him. And of course he would be helping the skipper at the same time. But–

He picked up a twig and broke it carelessly. It was fun back on the Angle too. His Dad was counting on him to help guide fishermen the next three months, and he had been planning on the money that he'd make doing it. He'd need every cent he could save to help pay his expenses at school. He couldn't make much money helping Mr. Harmon, that was sure. The skipper couldn't afford to pay very much.

"I don't know of anyone I'd rather have with me," Bil

continued. "I wouldn't have to worry about handling the *Valiant* if you were along. You know just what to do."

"Maybe your uncle wouldn't want me."

"Leave that to me," his friend said firmly. "Just say the word and I'll fix it up with Uncle Jim."

"You'd better wait awhile," Danny countered. I'd have to talk with my parents first."

There was nothing to do until the following morning when the *Valiant* went out. The boys sauntered down to the river that afternoon, swam awhile, and lay on their backs in the sun waiting for dinner and 8 o'clock so they could pick up their dates.

"I ought to let you go with both girls, Bill," Danny said dourly. "You could at least have asked me before you had Evelyn line up a date for me."

"Quit crabbing! You'll change your tune when you see the girl she's got for you."

They got up and started toward Bill's home.

"What are we going to do tonight?" Danny asked his companion.

"We'll just mess around for a while," Bill said. "I suppose we'll wind up going down to the dock to watch the boats or take in the skating rink or just sit in the shop and talk."

When eight o'clock came they went over to Evelyn's house where the girls were waiting. Evelyn came to the door and let them in. A short, round-faced girl with a heavily painted face and two chins was standing behind her.

"I want you to meet Glenna Borglund," Evelyn said to Danny.

The girl giggled self-consciously.

"How do you do?" Danny said.

They went into the house and sat in the living room for a few minutes talking casually. Finally Bill turned to Evelyn. "Well, what sounds good for tonight?"

"Oh," Glenna broke in, giggling again, "we could go to a movie maybe. There's a good one at the theater tonight. And then–."

"That's old stuff," Evelyn broke in. "I'm tired of going to the movies. How about it, Bill? Did you ask your uncle if we could use the *Valiant* tonight?"

He looked flustered. "No," he answered, "I didn't get a chance to talk to Uncle Jim about it, but I'm sure that I could fix it up with him. What's on your mind?"

"There's the sweetest dance out at Point Loma Resort about ten miles down the lake," she answered, her face lighting. "It's only for teenagers. Nobody out of their teens can go, and they've got a super band from the Cities and everything. I've never been there but everyone says that it's the best."

"That sounds wonderful," Glenna cooed. She turned and fastened her baby-blue eyes on Danny. "Doesn't it sound super to you?"

It wasn't that she was large that irked Danny. He had known a lot of large girls back in Cedarton who were great. But why did she have to giggle all the time? And why did she talk like a dunce?

Danny looked over at Bill questioningly, asking with his eyes whether or not Bill had known what was coming.

"Doesn't that sound super, Danny?" Glenna continued, leaning over and touching him on the arm with her pudgy fingers. He drew away. "They've got a super floor out there. It's just–it's just super."

"Why don't you phone your Uncle Jim, Bill?" Evelyn asked, that pleading tone coming back to her voice again. "And ask him about letting us use the boat. It's such a beautiful evening. The ride down to Point Loma would be so wonderful." Her prettiest, most winsome smile came out to charm him. "I'll call some of the other kids and we can have a regular party on the boat."

Bill looked over at Danny miserably. "I–" he began.

"I'm sorry, but I'm afraid that you'll have to count me out," the Orlis boy said, his voice firm and even.

Evelyn was contemptuous. "Now what's the matter with you?" she asked sarcastically. "Have you got a broken leg?"

"I was telling you about Danny," Bill broke in. "You remember, don't you? He doesn't dance."

"Oh, but I just love to teach people to dance!" Glenna said. She giggled again. "It's so much fun. You go along, Danny, and Evelyn and I both will be your teachers. We'll dance with you as many times as you want to."

"What Bill means," Danny said, "is that I don't care to dance. You see, I'm a Christian and I feel that it's better for me not to dance."

"I go to church too," Glenna snapped irritably. "But I never heard anything so ridiculous. There's nothing wrong with going to a good, clean dance."

"Every person has got to decide for himself what he's going to do and what he's not going to do," Danny told her. "The Bible tells us that we are to present our bodies as a living sacrifice to the Lord Jesus. It also says that we're supposed to avoid the very appearance of evil. I've been in a dance hall a few times, and I know that I wouldn't want to take Jesus there. So I figure that it's better for me not to dance."

She eyed him quizzically. "What sort of a fanatic are you anyway?"

"I don't know," he answered, grinning. "What sort of a fanatic would you call me?"

"Bill used to have a bunch of screwy ideas like that when I first started going with him, Glenna," Evelyn explained to her girl friend, "but I've been working on him. He soon found out that he'd have to get rid of a lot of that corny religion of his if he was going to go out with me."

Danny glanced at his friend. Bill's face was coloring slightly.

"I don't think I could get the boat tonight anyway," he said lamely, "now that I think of it. Danny and I got it all ready for the trip back out to the Angle tomorrow. We loaded in a lot of lumber and cement. It wouldn't be clean enough for us to use, even if Uncle Jim would let us take it."

A strange, determined look came over her face.

"Well," she said, her voice rising, "it will have to be all right this time. But I want you to know one thing. You're going to take me to the next teen dance over at Loma or I'm going to know the reason why."

"Well," he said numbly, "we'll see about that when the time comes."

"We'll see about it right now," she retorted. She got up quickly and went into the other room and consulted a calendar. "It's the last Saturday night in July. You're going to get the boat and take us to Point Loma."

"I'll see," Bill answered.

"If you want to keep going out with me, Bill Marsh," she announced firmly, "you'd better take me. I'm tired of all this kid stuff. I want to go where we can have some real fun."

There was a long, awkward silence.

Finally the Orlis boy said, "Why don't we go down to the pier? There ought to be a lot of the kids down there tonight."

Evelyn snorted her opinion of his suggestion. "Who wants to go down there?" she asked. "Only the boring kids will be there. The others will all be out at Point Loma having a wonderful time."

"How about going down and watching for a while anyway?" Bill asked. "Then we can go over to the shop and get a sandwich or some ice cream."

"I think I'd like a chocolate sundae," Glenna said,

smacking her lips, "with peanuts and marshmallows on top."

"I suppose we might as well," Evelyn said, pouting. "There's nothing else to do."

They went down to the pier and watched the boats for half an hour or so, then over to the shop, but the evening didn't go off the way they had planned. It was scarcely 10 o'clock when the girls insisted on going home.

"This sure turned out to be a bust." Bill said as he and the Orlis boy walked back toward his home.

"I'm sorry that I ruined it for you, Bill," Danny said, "but you know how I stand on things like dancing. If you'd just told me what Evelyn wanted to do, I would have stayed at home."

"I know," his friend said shortly.

"I'm sorry too that you've started dancing," Danny went on. "That's one thing I sure didn't figure you'd do."

"I haven't been going to many," Bill said, "alibiing." "And when I do go, I only dance two or three times. The only reason I go at all is to take Evelyn. She enjoys dancing so much."

"It's awfully hard on your Christian testimony, Bill," the Orlis boy said softly.

"I wish you'd quit preaching at me! I'm all right! I know what I'm doing!"

CHAPTER 5

FOLLOWING AFAR

It was a cool, crisp evening and Danny and Bill walked briskly down the darkened street toward home. Neither of them spoke. They went up on the porch together and into the house.

At the stairs Danny paused.

"Well," he said, "good night."

"Good night, Danny," his friend said warmly. He started toward his bedroom, then stopped and came back. "I–I'm sorry I flew off like that. I sure didn't have any reason for doing it."

"That's okay," Danny said, smiling. "I'll see you in the morning."

"And, Danny," Bill continued, "I haven't really drifted away from the Lord, even if you think I have. I love Him as much as I ever did. I just see some things a little more sensibly, that's all."

Before the Orlis boy could answer, Bill had gone up the stairs.

That night Danny prayed for a long while about his friend. He prayed that Bill would again see that a Christian should live a life of holiness, and that he would quit doing those things that were getting between him and the Lord.

The boys were up at six the following morning and had breakfast. Even though the schedule didn't call for them to leave Warroad before 8 o'clock they had to be at the dock an hour early to help fishermen load their gear and get the *Valiant*'s powerful new motor warmed up.

They were just getting into their jackets when Bill's aunt came hurrying over to see them.

"Oh, there you are, Billy!" she said. "I'm so glad that I got here before you left."

"Why?" he asked quickly. "What's wrong? How's Uncle Jim?"

"I think he must be a little better," she replied. "And he says that he feels fine. But the doctor has told us that he shouldn't be out on the boat for at least three months."

The boys said nothing.

"Your uncle and I talked it over," she continued. "We've got to get someone to help you on the *Valiant*, Bill. Do you think that your friend could handle it?" She turned to Danny. "We couldn't afford to pay very much, and you might not want to work for what we could give you, but we need help so badly that I thought I'd come over and ask."

Danny was silent. Bill and his parents and Mrs. Harmon were watching him intently.

"Perhaps," he thought, "if I go on the boat with Bill, I'd have a chance to talk with him while we're out together. Maybe I could get him to see that he's out of fellowship with God when he's living in the world."

"I'll have to talk to Dad," he said at last. "He's counting on having me guide for him this summer. But if he says that it's all right, I'll do it."

A big smile broke across the elderly woman's face. "I knew that the Lord would work out things for us," she said confidently. "I told Uncle Jim that we didn't have to worry. God would take care of us."

Suddenly Danny felt warm and good all over.

It was agreeable with his parents for him to help on the *Valiant* until Jim Harmon was able to go back.

"I'm glad that you're going to help Jim, Danny," Carl Orlis said. "You'll be home every other night."

"The only thing, Carl," Mrs. Orlis put in, "is your sister's boy who's coming from Toledo in July. We'll want to show him a good time."

"Maybe the skipper will be well enough by the time Richard gets here so that Danny won't have to help him then," Carl replied.

* * *

The days on the little packet boat passed swiftly. Business held up surprisingly well. They lost a little trade right at first when timid fishermen or tourists came down and looked at the small boat and saw that it was being piloted by two teenaged boys. But as the weeks passed, business began to pick up until they were doing almost as much as Mr. Harmon would have done.

"I'll tell you, boys," the skipper said after a very successful Fourth of July excursion, "you'll never know how much this means to my wife and me. We'd have really been in a bad way if you hadn't taken over for us."

"We're so glad that we could help you," they told him.

"Next week I'll make the final payment on the new motor," the skipper said. "Then we'll start to lay up a little nest egg for winter." He looked across at his wife and winked. "The way I feel I don't think that it will be too long until I'm able to take over the *Valiant* myself."

"You'd just as well let us handle it, Uncle Jim," Bill said. "We're getting along fine."

"And," Danny answered, "we're having a lot of fun besides."

Several times when there were no passengers aboard, Danny Orlis tried desperately to talk with Bill about the Lord Jesus.

"But I tell you, I believe the same way as I always have," his friend countered, "and I'm not living in sin. I'm just being sensible. That's all."

"The Bible tells us that there is a certain way we ought to live," Danny said. "Do you honestly feel that you're living a holy Christian life?"

"I'm living just as close to God as I ever did," Bill argued. "There isn't a single thing I'm doing that is really, honestly hurting me in a spiritual way."

"Well," the Orlis boy continued, "do you still attend Sunday school and church?"

Bill bit his lower lip. "Sometimes."

"Youth group?"

He shook his head. "We've gone all over that, Danny," he said irritably. "You know that Evelyn won't go places like that with me, and besides the meetings got so they weren't interesting anymore."

"How about your daily devotions?" the Orlis boy asked. "You used to read your Bible regularly every day. Do you still do that?"

"Most of the time."

"Did you read it yesterday or the day before or any time this week?"

"No," Bill admitted sheepishly.

"How about last week and the week before that?" Danny persisted. "Did you have your devotions any time during that period?"

"I don't see what that's got to do with living close to the Lord," Bill said. "I've been too busy to have devotions this summer. You know that."

Danny was silent for a long while.

"You got too busy about the time you started going out with Evelyn, didn't you, Bill?" he asked softly.

His friend flushed scarlet but said nothing.

Bill talked very little about his girlfriend after that. He still went out with her as often as before, but he said nothing about her to Danny. And he made no attempt to get the Orlis boy to go along with him on another double date. Danny wrote Kay about what had happened and asked her to pray for Bill.

"The crazy guy lets this Evelyn twist him around her little finger," he wrote. "Believe me, a Christian certainly has no business going out with someone who isn't saved, even for a little while. It really makes it rough for him to continue to live a holy life."

Danny had almost forgotten about the teen dance until Evelyn came down to the dock to talk with Bill about it the week before it was to take place.

"You haven't forgotten that we've got a date for the last Saturday night in July, have you?" she said.

He flushed. "Nope," he told her. "I haven't forgotten."

"I just wanted to check on it," she continued. "A bunch of the kids were talking about it at the shop last night. They all wanted to go, but none of them have a way. I told them that you were planning on taking the *Valiant*, and they thought that was a great idea. We can have a real party."

"That sounds like fun," Bill replied.

"You'd better talk to your uncle about it right away," she said, "so that we'll know what to count on."

Then she turned to Danny. "I don't suppose you'll be there," she said sarcastically.

"I'm not planning on it," he told her as kindly as he could.

"You ought to. You know you might surprise yourself at how much fun you'll have if you'd just get out of your shell. Just look at Bill. He used to be a real bore before I got hold of him. Now he has as much fun as anybody." With that she turned and walked away.

"I certainly wish you weren't going to that dance, Bill," the Orlis boy said when Evelyn was out of hearing range.

"I'd like to have you go along just once, Danny," Bill countered. "Just once, so you'd actually know what goes on over there. It's not so bad, really. It's not nearly as bad as you think. Like Evelyn says, if you'd just go with us, you'd find out that you can have a lot of fun. And you can be a better testimony to the rest of our friends. None of them want to get mixed up in anything that's so dull and so–so fanatical."

The Orlis boy shook his head. "Nope, Bill, I can't see it."

* * *

Back at the Angle, Danny tried to help Ron and Roxie in their efforts to bring the Douglass youngsters to Christ. He took the four of them fishing on the afternoons he and Bill were at the Angle and talked with them about their souls.

"You know, Pete," he said to the Douglass boy one afternoon, "I can't quite understand you. You seem to be interested in Jesus. You bring the subject up every time that we're together. You say that you know you're a sinner, and that you need to take the Lord Jesus Christ as your Savior, but you don't want to yield your heart to Him."

"I–I know," Pete said, stammering.

Danny leaned forward intently. "Why not?" he asked.

"I'd like to," the boy said. "I really would, Danny. Only I–I can't."

"Why can't you?"

"I just can't. That's all."

They stayed out fishing for at least two hours after that, but Pete wouldn't speak to Danny or even look at him. And when they let him out of the boat, he scrambled off the dock and up to the log house without even waiting to take his fish.

Danny sat there shaking his head.

"I could just cry," Roxie said tenderly. "I was hoping that we could lead him to Christ. Ron and I have been praying for Pete and Ellen every night."

"Just keep on praying," Danny told her, "and witness to them every chance you get."

* * *

On the Tuesday night before the teen dance at Point Loma, Danny and Bill were at the Angle.

"It's Bible Club tonight, Danny," Ron told him. "Would you like to go up to the Douglass farm with us to get the kids?"

"Sure thing."

When they reached the little log house Mrs. Davis came to the door. The Orlis boy hadn't seen her since they brought her up the day he and the twins came home from school the month before.

"Now what do you want, young man?" she demanded dourly.

"We are having Bible Club down at our place tonight," Danny told her. "We came up after Pete and Ellen."

"Bible Club?" she echoed. "Is that where they've been getting all that foolishness? The past few weeks all they've been able to talk about has been sin and Satan and needing a Savior."

"I'm sure they've heard the Gospel there," Danny said, "although I've only been at a couple of meetings myself."

Mrs. Davis's eyes narrowed. It seemed that a cloud passed over her face.

"They aren't going!" she snapped. "We're not going to tolerate any more of that stuff around here! Now I want you to leave, and don't come back!"

Roxie squeezed Danny's arm hard.

"Did you hear me?" Mrs. Davis repeated. "Don't you dare set foot on this land again! We're not tolerating any more of this foolishness!"

A CHAPERON FOUND

Mrs. Davis stood there for a moment or two, staring belligerently at Danny and the twins. Then she stepped back and reached for the door to close it. She slammed it so violently that a long strip of cement chinking fell from between the logs above it.

Ron took hold of Danny's arm and turned. "Come on, Danny," he said quickly. "She's awfully mad. Let's beat it before she comes out again!"

"She's not going to hurt us."

He walked back to the *Scappoose* with the twins. Roxie's hands were trembling on the oar as she and Ron pushed the boat out into midstream. And she was blinking rapidly to keep back the tears.

"There now, Roxie," Danny said, "everything's going to work out all right. Don't feel so badly."

"But, Danny," she said, "I know that Pete and Ellen are almost ready to trust Jesus as their Savior. Ron and I have been talking and talking and talking to them. If it weren't for Mrs. Davis, I know they would accept the Lord." She paused and rubbed at her eyes. "It–it makes me so mad I could cry."

"That isn't going to do any good, Roxie," Danny replied. "We've all been praying for them. Don't you believe that God can handle Mrs. Davis? Don't you think that He can lead Peter and Ellen to Himself?"

She nodded, wiping at her eyes again.

"Then why don't we pray a little harder and stop all this worrying?" Danny continued. "God can work things out, and He will in His own time. We've got to have faith."

"I–I'll try, Danny," she managed. "But I–I do want Pete and Ellen to become Christians."

Back at home Danny talked with his dad about what had happened.

"I don't know what the real trouble is with Mrs. Davis," Carl Orlis said. "Somebody told me that he'd heard Douglass say that his sister had been a regular church-goer years ago, but he never did hear him say what had happened to change her. It must have been something bad that would cause her to be so bitter against the Lord."

"Would you and Mom pray for the Douglass kids, Dad?" Danny asked. "If it weren't for her influence, I know that they could be reached for Christ."

Carl Orlis nodded. "And," he said, "we don't want to forget Mrs. Davis either."

The next trip back to the Angle for the *Valiant* was

on the day before the big dance. When they pulled in to the Orlis dock, Bill washed down the deck and shined the windows until they were so clean they looked as though there wasn't any glass in them.

"So you're really going tomorrow night," Danny said, the disappointment plain in his voice.

"I don't know," Bill answered uncomfortably. "I thought I'd clean up the old tub though, just in case I do decide to go."

Danny turned and walked slowly back to the house. That night Bill seemed to avoid him, and the Orlis boy went up to bed.

Early the next morning, before they had even finished breakfast, a boat pulled up to the dock and Mrs. Davis climbed painfully up onto the Orlis dock.

"I'm going to town with you," she announced to Danny and Bill. "I really should wait until tomorrow when the other boat makes its trip, but I've got some trading to do." She turned and moved slowly toward the back of the *Valiant*.

Danny hurried to help her in, but she brushed him away. "When I need your help, young man," she snorted, "I'll ask for it."

The sky was gray and threatening as they pulled out of Pine Creek and headed up the bay toward American Point.

"I wish you'd go along with us tonight, Danny," Bill said. "If you'd just go once, you'd find out all the fun you're missing."

"No chance."

"Come on. If you go and don't like it, you can always go back to the *Valiant* and hang out until we go home. You won't have to stay at the dance unless you want to."

Danny shook his head. "No, thanks!" he said. "We've gone all over this a dozen times, Bill. I'll have to get along without that sort of fun, I guess."

Mrs. Davis straightened.

"You mean that you've got a chance to go to a dance," she echoed, "and you're not taking it. What on earth's the matter with you, boy!"

Bill was at the wheel and Danny went back to where Mrs. Davis was sitting.

"I'm a Christian," he told her simply, using the same words he had used on Bill, "and I feel that it's better for a Christian not to go places where he can't take Christ with him."

"But I might need you to help run the boat, Danny," Bill countered. "Certainly you could go along and help me do that. That wouldn't hurt you."

Danny Orlis got to his feet and looked out at the black, rolling clouds.

"From the way this weather looks," he said almost hopefully, "nobody will get to go. Your uncle wouldn't want you to take the *Valiant* out if a storm were coming up."

"We'll worry about that when it starts to storm," Bill replied confidently. He grinned at his companion. "We're going to have a big time, Danny. You'd better change your mind and go along with us. I can get a great date for you."

The Orlis boy stepped closer to the helm. "Bill," he said softly, "doesn't the Lord mean anything to you anymore? Don't you care what God wants you to do?"

For an instant the color fled from Bill's face, and he looked quickly away.

"Don't you care about living the way Christ wants us to live, Bill?" Danny persisted. "Doesn't that matter to you anymore?"

Bill Marsh faced him, his eyes blazing.

"Listen, you!" he snapped angrily. "I've had all the preaching that I'm going to stand for. I'll do what I please, go where I please, and when I please. And neither you nor anybody else is going to stop me!"

He turned back to the wheel and for the rest of the trip didn't speak to Danny. The Orlis boy went through his tasks mechanically, a dull, heavy ache in his heart.

Mrs. Davis moved closer to Bill. "If I were just twenty years younger," she said, "I'd give a pretty price to go along to that dance with you. If there's anything that I love, it's a good, lively dance."

When they pulled into the dock on the Warroad River, Evelyn and two other girls were there waiting for them.

"Oh, Bill!" she wailed. "The most awful thing has happened. I got eight couples lined up to go with us tonight. And now our mothers say that we can't go unless there's a chaperon along."

"Wow, that's tough." He cast a quick, sidelong glance at Danny to see whether or not the Orlis boy was smiling.

"It isn't that we mind the idea of a chaperon," she went on, "but we've hunted over the whole town, and we can't find anyone who's free tonight."

By this time Mrs. Davis had hobbled out to the back of the boat. "Chaperon?" she asked. "Did I hear somebody say you had to have a chaperon before you could go to the dance? If you don't mind an old lady along, I'll chaperon for you."

"You would?" Bill echoed. "That'll be great."

She looked over at Danny and smiled. "Sure you don't want to go along, young man?" she asked. "We'll have a great time!"

Danny Orlis's heart sank as he turned his attention to the freight.

The sky had been dark and threatening all afternoon, but along toward evening the clouds broke up and the sun was a ball of fire as it dropped behind the western horizon.

Bill hurried through dinner and went upstairs to dress for the dance. When he came down, he hurried past Danny.

"I'll be home late, Mom," he called. "Don't wait up for me." It was only 7:30, but he had to get Evelyn and meet the rest of the kids. Then it would take an hour to get the *Valiant* out to Point Loma. The dance would be started when they got there, even if he hurried.

Danny read for a few minutes, then picked up his jacket and went over to the church to youth group. The program they had arranged for the evening was good enough, but for some reason he could not get his mind on it. He kept thinking of Bill and the other kids on the *Valiant* headed for the dance.

There was a great deal of business to transact at the meeting that night, and when it was finally over it was almost 10 o'clock.

"Come on," one of the guys said to him. "Let's go down to the shop and have a sandwich and some ice cream."

He started to refuse as they stepped out of the church, but he stopped suddenly.

"What was that?" he asked.

"What was what?"

"I thought I saw lightning off in the west."

"Sure," the other boy replied. "It was flashing some when I came in about 8:15. The barometer's been dropping all day. The news says that we're in for a real storm before morning."

"I sure hope not," Danny answered fervently.

"What are you so worried about, Danny?" one of the guys asked him. "You're not out on the lake tonight. You're right here in Warroad, and I don't think that we're going to blow away."

"No," the Orlis boy said weakly, "I'm not out on the lake, but I know somebody else who is out there tonight. I just hope he has sense enough to head in."

He shivered although the night was warm. Bill Marsh was out there on the *Valiant* without anyone who knew anything about either the boat or the lake to help him. Probably none of them had ever been out on the Big Traverse in a bad storm. Come to think of it, Bill had only run down to Point Loma a time or two. He didn't know the reefs or the channel down that way.

"Maybe they'll get off the lake before the storm hits."

"We'll have to pray that they do," Danny said, more to himself than his friends.

Danny hadn't intended to go to the shop with the rest of the kids. He had been up since five that morning, and he was tired. But he went with them now, trying to watch the storm as it approached and to gauge the speed with which it was coming up. The lights from town made it difficult.

It hadn't seemed that the clouds were moving fast at all, and he began to relax a little when there was a soft patter of rain, followed by a tense, breathless hush.

"Here it is!" he exclaimed.

"You don't call this a storm, do you?" one of his friends asked.

"You just–." He didn't get to finish what he was saying. There was a sudden rush of wind, and the rain came cascading down.

"Come on!" somebody shouted. "Let's make a dash for it!"

They started to run for the shop across the street.

In the few seconds it took them to cross, their clothes were soaked.

"I didn't know that it could rain so hard." One of them exclaimed.

Danny stood there watching the wind and the rain while the others went back to the booths and sat down. Half an hour or so later the telephone rang, and the owner of the shop answered it.

"Did any of you guys go over to Point Loma to the dance on the *Valiant* this evening?" he called over his shoulder.

They all shook their heads.

"Why?" Danny Orlis asked.

"They got scared of the storm and left there an hour and a half ago. Told the manager they'd report here when they got in, so he'd know that they were all right."

Danny's heart started hammering!

CHAPTER 7

A THRILLING RESCUE

The guys sat there for a minute or so listening intently to the storm and the halting conversation of the owner on the phone.

Danny felt the color drain from his cheeks and the palms of his hands moistened. The wind was roaring with renewed fury now, and they could hear the heavy seas hammering against the breakwaters, although the lake was several blocks away.

Finally, the shop owner came back up front, wiping his hands nervously. "I don't know what to think," he said. "The manager of the resort at Point Loma said this whole bunch of kids came in about nine o'clock and had only danced a little while when the clouds started coming up so fast that they got into the boat and headed back. He tried to get them to wait until the storm was over, but the kid who had the boat said he couldn't wait." The owner paused for a moment and stared out into the driving rain. "I wouldn't want to be out on the big lake in that!"

The guys turned to Danny. "The only boat a kid might have would be the *Valiant*," one of them said. "Was it, Danny? Did Bill take a bunch of kids to Point Loma to the dance?"

He nodded numbly.

"I knew something like this was going to happen when he started to go out with Evelyn," somebody exclaimed. "We haven't been able to get him to go to youth group or Sunday school or anything Christian since he began to date her."

"I didn't think Mr. Harmon would let Bill take the *Valiant* to go to a dance," somebody else put in. "He doesn't believe in that sort of thing."

"Maybe he didn't know anything about it," the boy sitting beside Danny said. "Maybe Bill took the boat without permission!"

Danny scarcely heard what they were saying. Only he really knew how dangerous the Lake of the Woods would be. Only he had been out in the center of the Big Traverse when dark, deep-troughed combers were slamming into the boat one after another, straining the heavy oak timbers until they groaned under the savage blows.

Perhaps he should have gone along with Bill. He wouldn't have had to dance. He could have waited there and helped get the *Valiant* safely back to Warroad. Perhaps – even as he thought, he knew that Bill was the one who had been wrong. But there wasn't time to think about that now. The sturdy little craft might be on the rocks or sinking! He got up quickly and started toward the door.

"Where are you going, Danny?" one of his friends called.

"I've got to see a guy!" he exclaimed. With that he zipped his jacket and plunged out into the storm.

The wind tore at his pants and jacket and lashed him with rain, but he scarcely felt it as he ran. Tom Galloway was the skipper of the Booth Fisheries' boat, the *Morton J. Webb*. And she was in that night. He had seen her tied up at the dock scarcely three hours before.

"O Lord Jesus," he prayed as he ran, "help Tom to be at home and agree to go with me after the *Valiant*. Make him go, Lord! And keep the kids safe!"

Tom was in bed when Danny got to his house, but he got into his clothes hurriedly and put on his raincoat and hat.

"This is going to be a bad go, Danny," he said quietly as he tried his powerful electric lantern. "Think maybe I'd better get Red out to help me."

"I can help," Danny put in quickly. "I–I don't think there's time to get anyone else. Bill doesn't know anything about the channels down that way. He's apt to be on the rocks!"

"The lunkhead!" Tom said mildly. "Anybody ought to know they shouldn't be out at night in strange waters – especially with the barometer falling and the storm warnings up."

Tom and Danny drove down to the docks and started the diesel in the *Morton J. Webb*. The wind was angling across the lake, piling big breakers into the river.

"Boy, it's going to be tough turning around in this, isn't it?" Danny shouted.

"You can say that again."

Danny loosed the bow line and Tom reversed the screw to back out into the river. Slowly, carefully, he brought her about until the prow was splitting the breakers, sending spray spuming along the deck.

"The first thing is to get out of the river without piling into anything," the captain muttered under his breath.

The powerful spotlights stabbed a tiny hole in the storm-riven night.

The storm was worse than Danny had supposed. The waves were piling over the cabin and the steel-hulled *Webb* was creaking and groaning under the strain.

"It's going to take us quite a while, Danny," Tom Galloway explained. "We've got to cut our speed to half throttle in seas like these."

Danny nodded silently. "O Lord Jesus," he prayed, "be with the kids on the *Valiant*! Keep them from harm! And–and watch out for Mrs. Davis too–" He choked up suddenly until he couldn't find words to pray. A big lump welled in his throat, and he swallowed hard.

He bit his lip savagely and grabbed for support as the *Webb* lurched over a huge, white-laced roller and wallowed crazily in the trough that followed, while the next sea piled over her.

"Keep watching, Danny," Tom cautioned. "They might have lost the running lights, or the battery might go dead if the motor quit on them. It'd be awfully easy to pass right by them on a night like this!"

Almost as he spoke Danny saw the weak, blinking light off the port bow. It was so faint that for an instant he wasn't sure that he had really seen it. He sucked in his breath sharply as he saw it once more.

"Tom!" he cried. "Look! Look!"

The grizzled boat captain turned momentarily and stared hard into the darkness. And then it came again.

"S-O-S" he spelled, reading the Morse code as it flashed. "S-O-S"

"It's them!" Danny cried. "It's them! It's got to be!"

Tom Galloway did not answer him as he brought the *Morton J. Webb* about and headed toward the weak distress signal.

"They're powerful close to a reef," he said more to himself than to his companion. "If they're actually on it we'll probably get in a jam too when we move in to get a line on them."

Danny's heart was hammering wildly as he leaned forward, trying to part the pitch darkness with his eyes. The waves were throwing the *Webb* more violently than ever as the skipper maneuvered closer to the signaling light.

"Take the wheel, Danny," he said at last, reaching for his electric lantern. "W-H-O A-R-E Y-O-U W-H-A-T I-S Y-O-U-R T-R-O-U-B-L-E"

The other boat signaled, "S-O-S S-O-S"

"What's the matter with him?" Tom stormed.

"That must be Bill," Danny answered. "All he knows of the Morse code is S-O-S."

"It's a wonder he knew that!"

He brought the *Webb* closer to the stranded boat, now moving even more cautiously, his ear tuned for the telltale scraping of the hull on rocks. He moved so close by that they could make out the darkened hull of the other craft tossing aimlessly on the water.

"Ahoy!" he called through the megaphone as he had Danny cut the motor momentarily. "Ahoy, the *Valiant!*"

"Ahoy!" a frightened voice shouted back.

"What's the trouble?"

"Motor quit!" It was Bill. Danny could recognize his voice. "Everybody's seasick!"

"Are you on the rocks?"

"We were, but we must have drifted off them."

"We're putting a line aboard! Get ready to make it fast!"

Danny's breath was coming in short, quick gasps as Tom took the wheel and brought the *Webb* so close to the *Valiant* the two boats almost brushed. For a split second they hung there close together. At that instant Danny heaved the line and it went sailing into the *Valiant*.

"We've got her, Tom!" he called jubilantly. "We've got her!"

Somehow Bill and his friends got the line secured to the prow of the *Valiant*, hoisted the anchor, and the *Webb* moved off slowly with the smaller boat in tow. Danny stood there in the stern of the Booth Fisheries' boat watching the taut line and the dark, sluggish hull behind them.

"O heavenly Father," he prayed thankfully, "thank You for being with the kids tonight even though they were dishonoring You by what they were doing. Help them to see what it is to be Christians if they don't know. And if they do, help them to see how they should live to honor You. And again, thank You for Your mercy. Amen."

The storm was still raging when they pulled into the river and manipulated the helpless *Valiant* up to her dock.

"Thanks, Tom!" Danny said fervently. "Thanks a lot!"

"Forget it," the *Webb*'s skipper replied. "Harmon would have done the same for me."

By this time the kids were getting off the *Valiant*, one by one. Bill came over to where Danny was standing. "Danny!" he exclaimed. "I might have known."

"Had sort of a rough night, didn't you?" the Orlis boy said grinning.

"I don't feel much like joking, Danny," Bill replied. "I was never so scared in my life. We got on those rocks for a couple of seconds before we dropped anchor. If we'd stayed on them much longer, we'd have pounded a hole in the bottom of the *Valiant* and we'd all have gone down."

It was still raining hard, but nobody seemed to mind the rain.

"Let's go someplace where we can talk, Danny," Bill continued earnestly. "I–I've got to talk to you!"

"Sure thing," the young woodsman answered.

"I've been wrong about so many things," Bill said.

CHAPTER 8

"A HEAP OF THINKING!"

For several minutes the kids all stood on the riverbank beside the boats, milling around aimlessly in the rain. Tom helped Mrs. Davis out of the *Valiant* and Danny rushed over to assist him. Her wrinkled face was drawn, and she shivered under Tom's heavy coat.

"I'd better get her down to the doctor's house and let him have a look at her," he said. "I'm afraid of pneumonia."

"I don't want to go to a doctor," she protested weakly. "I just want to go up to my hotel room and go to bed."

"We'll see what the doctor says first," Tom told her, as they helped her into the car. "Then we'll get you back to your hotel."

Mrs. Davis had said nothing to Danny at all, but as he turned to go she reached out impulsively and patted him on the arm.

"I'll get backed around," the captain of the *Webb* told Danny, "and then I'll take the kids home who live in the north end of town. The rest of you can get back in the boat and I'll pick you up in a jiffy."

"I don't know how I can ever thank you, Danny," Bill said when the two of them started back toward the *Webb*.

Evelyn came up just then and broke in before Danny could speak. "I want to go home," she said petulantly.

"We all do," Bill told her. "Mr. Galloway is going to haul all of us home in his car."

She grasped Bill by the hand. "Come on," she said. "Let's go on the first trip. I'm cold and wet and tired."

He shook his head. "Tom thought he ought to get Mrs. Davis to the doctor right away," he said. "So the kids who live up in that end of town are going first."

"I want to go on the first trip," she said. "Talk to him. Make him take me now." She coughed a little and shivered.

Bill shook his head. "I'm sorry," he said, "but you'll have to wait your turn. I've caused enough grief and trouble tonight. I'm not going to ask anyone for favors, especially Mr. Galloway. We can go inside the *Webb*. It's warm and dry there."

She stared at him, her eyes blazing. "I'm not going to set foot in a boat again tonight," she stormed. "If you won't see that I get home, and right away, I–I'll walk." She took half a dozen steps or so toward the railroad tracks, tiptoeing through the puddles that dotted the mud and cinder road.

"She shouldn't walk home in this rain," Danny said. "She'll catch an awful cold."

"She'll be back," Bill said shortly, "when she finds out that I'm not following her. That's been my trouble all along. I've been following her."

"We shouldn't blame others for the things that we do, Bill," Danny said gently.

Bill nodded his agreement.

They stood at the dock for a while, watching Evelyn. Once or twice she stopped and turned to see if they were coming after her. When she saw that they were not, she whirled and came plowing back through the mud, unmindful of the water puddles or her new suede shoes. She brushed past them hurriedly and sat down in the far corner of the boat cabin.

Later that night, after all the kids had been taken home, Danny and Bill finally tiptoed upstairs to their room.

"I want to get out of these wet clothes!"

Danny said softly. "I don't feel like I've been either dry or warm for a week."

"Me too!" Bill answered.

When they had gotten into their pajamas and crawled into their beds, Danny said, "You told me you had something you wanted to talk to me about. What was on your mind?"

Bill was silent for a long while. Finally he rolled over on his side and raised up on one elbow. "Danny," he said, "you remember how you warned me about missing youth group and Sunday school and church and messing around with the world?"

"Yes."

"I–I found out tonight how wrong I've been," he continued. "It happened before the storm, I think. I was miserable all the while we were going to Point Loma. The dance there wasn't fun. It was wicked. I had even left the building and had started back to the *Valiant* to wait until the others were ready to go home. That was when I noticed the storm clouds."

"I'm glad you see the way things really are," Danny said fervently. "Christ saved us from sin all right, but He expects us to live as though we are saved. He expects us to bear some fruit as Christians and we can't do that if we're living like the world."

"I wish I had taken your advice weeks ago," Bill said. "I know now how wrong it was for me to date Evelyn. She did everything she could to try to draw me away from the things of the Lord." He stopped awkwardly. "Now I've got to go and tell Uncle Jim that I took the *Valiant* to go to a dance instead of a picnic." He sighed deeply. "If I'd done as you wanted me to, I wouldn't have to do that now. I–."

"It doesn't do any good to look back," Danny said. "If we're ready to ask God's forgiveness and are ready to do what we can to make things right, He'll forgive."

Together they bowed their heads and prayed. When they finally finished Bill sat up in bed and switched on the light. His face was radiant.

"You know, Danny," he said hoarsely, "I feel much better now than I have since you came home. I was miserable most of the time you were along because you made me realize I was out of step with God."

Danny smiled at him happily.

The next morning early, they were sitting at the breakfast table when the phone rang for Danny.

"This is Mrs. Davis," the voice said shakily. "I want to talk to you right away."

"I–I'd like to," Danny told her, "but we're due to sail at eight o'clock and we've got a lot of work to do this morning before we can leave."

"Young man," Mrs. Davis bristled, "I want to talk to you *now*. It won't take but a few minutes, but it can't wait. I'm at the hotel." She hung up abruptly.

"What do you know about that!" Danny exclaimed.

"You go over and see her," Bill said, "and I'll go over and talk to Uncle Jim." He had already confessed to his folks.

"Okay," Danny answered, "but I sure can't figure this one out."

Mrs. Davis asked him in when he knocked on the door some fifteen minutes later. She was sitting in a rocking chair with a blanket drawn tightly about her shoulders. Her nose was red, and she daubed her eyes with a handkerchief.

"Shut the door," she said curtly, "and sit down over there."

Danny did as he was told.

When he had seated himself, Mrs. Davis half turned in her chair to face him. "Danny," she said, her voice breaking, "I've done a heap of thinking these past few hours. A heap of thinking!"

He squirmed nervously. "I was very sorry that you got so wet and cold and seasick last night," he told her. "We came just as soon as we found out you were stranded."

"That isn't what I wanted to talk to you about," she retorted. "I've been thinking about how different you are than the rest of those youngsters – how clean and fresh and–and decent you act, even to a cantankerous old woman."

"It's nothing I've done myself," Danny told her. "It's only that I've given myself to Jesus and put my trust in Him to help me live an honorable, Christian life."

Mrs. Davis started to speak again. Then she stopped and her eyes filled to brimming. "I know," she managed. "That's what I want to talk to you about." She leaned forward and lowered her voice. "I'm a Christian," she said, her voice breaking. "I know I haven't been acting like one these thirty odd years, but I am just the same. When my husband died, I became so bitter against God that I thought I hated Him." She swallowed hard. "That was the reason I took such a dislike to you. I knew that you were living the way I ought to."

"I'm afraid that I don't measure up on that living business, Mrs. Davis," Danny answered. "I don't live as close to the Lord as I'd like to."

She acted as though she hadn't even heard him. "I haven't been asleep all night," she said. "I've been reading a Bible and praying. Now I want to ask your forgiveness."

"Sure," Danny said uncomfortably, "I'll–I'll forgive you. I really don't have anything to forgive you for though."

"You'll never know how I talked about you and ridiculed you and–" she stopped short as she thought of something. "And the Douglass children. To think I stood in the way, keeping them from trusting Christ as their Savior. I'm going back to the Angle in a few days and I'm going to talk to them and tell them how wrong I've been. I know they'll come through!"

Danny's head was swimming as he left the hotel after half an hour and hurried down to the dock. Bill was already there.

"I got things fixed up with Uncle Jim," he said smiling, as soon as Danny approached. "And guess what! The doctor says that he can go back on the *Valiant* next Monday morning. Isn't that super?"

"I'll say it is," Danny exclaimed. "That's great! In fact, it's wonderful!"

THE GOSPEL COMES
TO FIRST CHURCH

CHAPTER 1

WORKING TOGETHER

Danny Orlis had been home for Christmas, and Tex Williams flew him back to Cedarton the day before classes were to start again at the Bible Institute. He had scarcely gotten off the plane and over to the Meyers' home when Chuck Martin called and asked him to come over to the Foresters'.

Mrs. Forester met him at the door.

"Danny," she said excitedly, "it's so wonderful to think that Marilyn and Charles are working together in our church. Dr. Carpenter, he's our pastor, you know – he was just here a few minutes ago and I'm so thrilled I just have to tell someone about it. He said that he's never had such an active youth group in any church he's ever served. And it's all because of Marilyn."

"That's great," Danny told her.

Marilyn, Chuck, and Kay were waiting for him in the basement recreation room.

"Now what's this all about?" he asked, sitting down beside Kay. "Marilyn's mother is sure excited about something."

"It's our work with the young people," Marilyn answered.

"And we're just as thrilled as she is," Chuck put in. "I tell you, Danny, it's been wonderful."

"That's why we wanted to get together tonight," the Forester girl continued. "We're having a special meeting tomorrow evening, and we decided to meet tonight and pray about it."

They sat attentively while Kay read a section from the Bible. Then they got down on their knees and asked God's blessing on the meeting the following night.

"It's all the more wonderful," Marilyn said when they had finished, "when we realize that the Gospel really isn't preached over there at all. And the kids are so eager to learn."

"Well!" Her mother's voice rasped harshly behind her. "I surely didn't expect to hear you criticizing Dr. Carpenter."

Marilyn flushed momentarily.

"I came down to see if you would like to have some sandwiches," Mrs. Forester went on coldly. "I certainly didn't expect to hear any talk like this."

"I'm sorry, Mother," Marilyn said, stammering. "I didn't mean to be criticizing the church or Dr. Carpenter. It's just that we're so excited about what's happening that–."

"I understand exactly what you mean."

The following evening the young people jammed into the basement of the church until Chuck and two of the boys had to bring in extra chairs. From the very beginning it was apparent that this service was going to be different. There was a different air about the singing, a different hush during Scripture reading and prayer. There was a different interest, a real heartfelt concern, as Chuck and Marilyn spoke.

It wasn't that they spoke any better. They didn't present any unusual truths. Nor was the Gospel presented any more clearly. But the interest of the kids was great, and when they finished, a tense, expectant hush fell over the entire group.

"Now," Chuck concluded, "if any of you would like to talk more about this matter, we'll be happy if you will come to either Marilyn or me. The decision to trust Christ as your Savior is very important. In fact it requires all of us – our hearts, our bodies, our very being. If you feel the weight of sin in your life tonight and want to get right with the Lord Jesus, just come and talk with us about it, won't you?"

When the service was over, tall, angular Claire Eaton came striding up to Chuck. His father, a lawyer, was one of the lay leaders in the church.

"I want to see you about this thing sometime, Chuck," he said earnestly. "There are some questions I don't understand about this sin question."

"We can talk now," Chuck replied, starting off toward one of the smaller rooms.

The younger boy hesitated. "I–I've got a date," he protested, "so I can't tonight. But I do want to talk to you. What you said sort of gets hold of a guy."

"It won't take more than a few minutes," Chuck insisted.

Claire looked toward the door.

"I'll see you tomorrow night." And then he was gone.

Chuck and Marilyn looked after him sorrowfully.

"We'll have to keep on praying for him, Marilyn," Chuck said. They left the church together and walked down the darkened, snow-packed street.

"Just think," she said dreamily, "if Claire could be brought to the Savior, there'd be a chance of bringing his dad and maybe influencing the entire church."

He grinned down at her. "We'd better take one step at a time, young lady," he said laughing.

They walked on together in silence.

"I know this," he continued after a time, "it's been great fun working with you."

She looked up at him. "It's been fun for me too." There was a new tenderness in her voice. "There's something about working together in the Lord's service that–

"That what?"

She colored slightly.

"That what?" he asked again.

"That seems to bring a couple close together," she finished lamely.

"It's strange," he said softly, "but I was just think-ing the same thing myself."

For a long while that night after Chuck had gone home and Marilyn was in bed, she tossed restlessly.

It was strange, the feeling she was beginning to have for Chuck. She had gone out with a number of other boys when she had been in high school. There were Tim, Rick, and a lot of others. She'd had a giddy, breathless feeling about each one of them in turn, thinking she would die if she didn't get to go out with them. But this feeling for Chuck Martin was still and deep, a warm, serene feeling that seemed to envelop her. It wasn't a thing that had come on all at once like a flash of lightning in a dark sky, but rather it had grown so slowly that now, since she was aware of it, it seemed as though she had always felt that way about him. Quietly she got out of bed and knelt to pray.

* * *

There was an interruption in youth group because of a big dinner at the church, and it was two weeks before they met again. Claire Eaton had promised Chuck that he would be around to see him. On the contrary, he seemed to be avoiding him.

"I'm so glad that we can have youth group again," Marilyn said as they approached the big stone building. "I've been praying and praying that Claire will be back tonight and with a receptive heart."

"The guy bothers me," Chuck said. "He seemed to be so eager to get right with the Savior. Yet he acts as though he's actually afraid. I got the idea that he's afraid he might have to give up something if he did."

Claire Eaton was at the meeting that night. He came in early and sat on the front row. Marilyn noticed that he brought his Bible.

It was her turn to lead the singing that evening. She did so fervently, and the kids threw back their heads and sang until they could be heard half a block away. They were enjoying it so much that she let them sing a few extra songs. They were just finishing when the door opened and Dr. Carpenter came in.

"I heard this beautiful singing," he broke in, "and I just had to come down and see what was going on. It's wonderful to hear young people lifting their voices to the glory of God."

He sat down in the back of the room, crossed his legs, and leaned against the wall. He said that he had come because of the singing, but as Chuck arose to speak he leaned forward intently.

"The most important thing in the world," the youthful speaker began, "is to get right with God. It can't be done by being good. The Bible tells us that there is none righteous. No, not one. It can't be done by attending church or Sunday school or youth group meetings. It can't be done by psychology or by saying to yourself every day that in every way you are getting better and better. Salvation comes only by recognizing that you are a sinner and need a Savior. It comes only by confessing your sin and putting your trust in the Lord Jesus Christ."

Dr. Carpenter leaned forward, listening intently to every word that was spoken. At first his thin, bony face was inscrutable. But as the youthful Bible school student continued to speak, his eyes began to flash, and his lips were hard set. When the meeting was finally over and the benediction was given, the pastor walked with determination up to the front. Claire Eaton intercepted him.

"I'd like to talk with you a moment, Dr. Carpenter," the boy said seriously. "I've been wanting to talk with someone about my religious life for the past couple of weeks. That talk tonight really got hold of me. Chuck made me feel as though I'm the worst sinner in the whole world."

The minister shook his head almost sorrowfully. Then he smiled down at Claire and patted him on the shoulder.

"Don't take that sort of thing too seriously, my boy," he said. "You a sinner? Why, you've been one of the most faithful boys in our Sunday school for years. And your father is the lay leader of our church. You don't have anything to worry about, Claire. You shouldn't let this emotionalism get you!"

CHAPTER 2

A DISTURBED PASTOR

The following morning, shortly after nine o'clock, Dr. Carpenter knocked on the door of the Forester home. Marilyn's mother went to open it, brusquely, annoyance in every move. Agents and salespeople ought to know they shouldn't be knocking on people's doors at such an hour. Well, they weren't going to sell her anything! With firm determination she jerked the door open. "I don't–" she said curtly. And then her eyes focused on Dr. Carpenter's neat gray suit. She stopped suddenly. A faint flush moved across her sagging jaw. "Oh, Dr. Carpenter," she exclaimed, "I didn't know it was you. I wouldn't have expected you so early."

"That's quite all right," he chuckled.

"If I had known I would at least have combed my hair," she apologized. "I don't know how long it's been since I went around the house like this."

The color came up into her cheeks as she uttered the lie.

"You should have seen Mrs. Carpenter when I left this morning," the pastor said amiably. "Curlers bristling like porcupine quills all over her head."

"You're so understanding, Dr. Carpenter."

They went into the living room and sat down. Ordinarily the minister visited a few moments or so and told her something humorous that had happened, but this morning the smile fled quickly from his face.

"I don't know quite how to begin, Mrs. Forester," he said.

She stiffened. "What do you mean?"

"I have tried to help Marilyn come to her senses," he went on. "And I must say that she and that young man have done a splendid job of interesting our young people."

Mrs. Forester caught her breath sharply.

"I could go into the details, but I don't want to hurt you. I must tell you this, however. They've been preaching their fanaticisms. And to make an unbearable situation they have almost succeeded in getting John Eaton's boy to make a fool of himself over religion. If I hadn't been at the meeting last night we might have had a situation that could lead to real trouble."

Mrs. Forester began to sniffle softly, dabbing at her eyes.

"John called me this morning before he went to work," the minister went on. "He was terribly upset. I told him I'd take care of the matter immediately."

Mrs. Forester got up and walked slowly across the room to another chair.

"What are you going to do?" Her voice was thin and hollow.

The minister took a deep breath.

"I realize what your position is," he said, "and I know you're aware of the fact that I'm very much concerned about it. I want nothing more than to bring Marilyn to her senses, but we can't permit things to go on as they are." He pursed his lips. "In fact, John Eaton insisted that I get in touch with him this afternoon and tell him what course of action I plan to take."

"Couldn't you talk with Marilyn and Charles?" Mrs. Forester asked at last. "Couldn't you make them see what this fanatical religion is doing to them – to everybody?"

"We'll give it some thought," he said, getting to his feet. "In the meantime, why don't you pray about it?"

* * *

Marilyn noticed during the next few days that her mother acted strangely toward her, but this time the older woman said nothing about it.

"Mom is acting so strangely again that it bothers me, Chuck," the girl confided. "She acts almost as she did back there a year or so right after Dad was saved."

"Perhaps she's under conviction herself," he replied hopefully. "You know how some people get when God is speaking to them."

"There have been so many times when we have been sure Mom was under conviction and nothing ever happened."

"Now, Marilyn," Chuck told her, "you know that you've been praying and so has your dad, Danny, Kay, and I. We've got to put our trust in the Lord. We can't run ahead of Him."

"But it's so hard to be patient. I just pray and pray and pray and don't see any sign of an answer."

"I guess that's where our faith comes in," Chuck said. "When we can see everything spelled out before us we don't have to have much faith. It's when we can't see ahead and still trust that we demonstrate our faith."

There was a long silence.

"I've been wondering about Dr. Carpenter," Chuck continued at last. "He certainly acted strangely the other night. He didn't say anything to us, but I had a feeling that he was going to come back and jump right down my throat."

"I really shook in my boots when you were talking about salvation and being 'born again' and the awfulness of sin while he was sitting back there listening."

"I couldn't see any point in changing what I had to say," Chuck replied. "After all, he's the pastor of the church. He's entitled to know what goes on in the youth group. And we certainly aren't ashamed of what we believe or the way we've been speaking."

"I know. But I can't help wondering what I'd have done if I'd been speaking when he came in. I don't know whether or not I'd have had the courage to go ahead the way you did."

"I didn't have it," Chuck admitted. "That all came from the Lord. I was so scared myself that I could hardly speak. But I just prayed silently, 'Lord Jesus, if You want me to give a good, strong testimony tonight with Dr. Carpenter sitting here, You're going to have to give me the words.'"

Marilyn sighed deeply. "I'm glad that your faith is so strong, Chuck," she told him. "I get strength just from being with you."

He started to speak but stopped and, taking her arm firmly, guided her across the street.

She was thrilled by the gentle touch of his powerful fingers. It was so different being with Chuck than any of the other guys with whom she had ever dated. It was soothing and warm and good just to be with him, to know that he was beside her.

"You know, Marilyn," he said at last, as though he weren't sure just how the words would sound, "it seems so good to be with you. I've gone out with many girls, and there have been a couple I thought a lot of, but somehow this is different."

She looked up at him and smiled. Suddenly it seemed as though a bond was forged between them, a quiet bond that was, even though unspoken, made with sinews of steel.

They didn't talk much as they walked home and sat in front of the big fireplace in the Forester home.

"Do you suppose it's the Lord's will for us to be more committed to each other?" he asked quietly.

Marilyn looked at him. His voice spoke vaguely of dating each other, but his eyes were far more eloquent.

"It's something I'd want to pray about," she replied quietly.

CHAPTER 3

AN INTERESTED SEEKER

Marilyn and Chuck continued with the youth work at First Church. They held the meetings as before, and the kids turned out in good numbers. Dr. Carpenter said nothing to them about the sort of messages they were bringing, but he was present at every meeting.

"I would like to have about five or ten minutes at the close of each service," he said to Chuck. "I think that the young people should hear from their pastor from time to time. And something that is particularly tailored for their needs. I don't want to interfere with your service at all. I'd just like the opportunity of bringing a few thoughts at the close of the meetings."

"Of course," Chuck answered.

That evening when Marilyn had finished the Bible study, Dr. Carpenter got to his feet.

"This matter of being 'born again,'" he said mildly,

"is a charming thought. It implies the new birth that comes to us with the warm spring rains. It implies all that is good and fine about our Christian faith. However, Christianity means more than that. At the time of Paul, the concept of being born again, or formally divorcing oneself from the old traditions, was necessary, because Christianity was new and struggling. Today we know that being a Christian is something more than confessing one's sin and accepting Christ as Savior. To be a Christian today is to strive to alleviate human suffering, to wipe out slums, to banish hunger from the earth." He paused and looked about. "I'm much more concerned how a member of our church feels about whether he has fulfilled the requirements for being born again. . . ."

Marilyn and Chuck sat there stunned, as though they could scarcely believe what they had heard. When the service was over, they went outside together.

"I don't like this at all, Marilyn," Chuck said when they were alone. "It seems to me as though Dr. Carpenter is deliberately trying to destroy everything that we've been doing."

"I feel sick inside."

"Do you suppose he'll be coming all the time?" Chuck asked. "If he does and speaks as he did tonight, there isn't much that we can do for the kids."

"And the pitiful part of it is," Marilyn went on, "some of them are so close to trusting the Lord Jesus as their Savior."

Chuck nodded.

"Did you see Claire Eaton's face tonight?" he asked. "Dr. Carpenter couldn't have hurt him more if he had slapped him in the face."

"What are we going to do, Chuck?" Marilyn asked.

"The first thing is to pray about it," he answered. "After all, Dr. Carpenter is the pastor there. If he's determined not to let us preach the Gospel in the meetings, there's not much that we can do."

During the following week Chuck and Marilyn spent a great deal of time together. Their activities at the church kept them busy one night a week in preparation, and they usually got together evenings to study.

Somehow the bond between them had grown swiftly. Neither of them mentioned it, but they almost instinctively began to spend more time together. And at least once a day Chuck found a reason to call her about something.

"We're beginning to see a great deal of that young man around here, Marilyn," Harold Forester laughed at the supper table one evening. "Do you suppose I ought to talk with him and see if his intentions are serious?" He managed to keep the smile from his face, but his eyes were twinkling.

Marilyn flushed a deep scarlet and Kay giggled sympathetically.

"Now, Harold," Mrs. Forester chided, "you know that you shouldn't tease Marilyn that way. Charles is a nice young man. I'm only too happy to see Marilyn going with him."

Marilyn looked up quickly, surprise on her face.

"I mean it," her mother went on. "He's kind and considerate and has good manners. And I know that when Marilyn is with him, we don't have to worry about her."

"Don't get me wrong," Harold Forester put in quickly. "I like Chuck too. The matter of fact is, if I were picking out a future son-in-law, I don't think I'd look any farther."

"Dad!" Marilyn protested indignantly.

Mrs. Forester's face clouded. "Really, Harold," she said coldly, "your sense of humor is quite warped. I'm sure that Marilyn has many plans which do not include Charles Martin."

Still blushing, Marilyn said nothing. Instead, what her mother had said set her mind to racing. It was true she had many plans for the future. But, although she had never realized it until that very moment, she came to see that somehow all of her plans did include Chuck Martin.

The Foresters were invited out for the evening, and Danny and Kay and the twins had just left to go down to the library to study when Marilyn had a call from Chuck.

"Claire Eaton just phoned," he said, his voice trembling with excitement. "He wants to talk with us right away. I told him to meet me at your place. I'll get there as quickly as I can. Be sure and keep him there if he happens to beat me."

As it turned out, the two boys reached the Forester home almost at the same time. Chuck was just taking off his coat when Claire came.

"I suppose you'll think it's silly that I want to talk with you," Claire began suddenly as he walked over to the fireplace and sat down in one of the chairs across from Marilyn. "I almost talked with Ron Orlis or Roxie, but I decided to see you."

For a moment or two Chuck and Marilyn sat there, waiting.

"What did you want to see us about?" Marilyn asked at last.

Claire swallowed hard.

"I just had to talk with you about this business of being born a second time," he said at last. "I've been thinking about what you said ever since you talked to me at youth group. I tried to understand Dr. Carpenter, but what he said doesn't match with what the Bible says. I haven't been able to sleep nights or do anything."

"There's a reason for that," Chuck said slowly, choosing his words with great care. "The Holy Spirit is speaking to you, Claire. And that's why you're so miserable. The Bible tells us that we all have sinned and come short of the glory of God, that we must put our trust in the Lord Jesus if we're to have salvation."

"That's the thing I haven't been able to understand. I've read those chapters you told me to read, but I can't figure out what they mean."

"Perhaps you're trying too hard, Claire," Chuck told him. "The Bible tells us that we must come to Him as a little child. There are some things we just can't understand. We have to take them on faith. Is it so hard then to trust the Lord Jesus? To take Him at His word?"

Claire shook his head uncertainly.

"What is it that bothers you?" Marilyn spoke softly.

Claire pursed his lips. "I don't really know," he confessed. "But I believe the thing that bothers me the most is that I'm not sure whether I could live a Christian life." His face grew even more serious. "I don't have any use for a hypocrite. What's more, I don't want to be one." He swallowed hard. "I–I want to be a Christian, Chuck, but I don't think I ever could live up to it."

"In a way, I'm glad to hear you say that," the older boy replied. "It shows that you realize there is something to this business of being a Christian besides making a profession. But the wonderful part of it is that you don't have to live up to it on your own. You couldn't live the way a Christian ought to. Neither can I, nor anyone else, in our own strength. But we can with the help of the Lord. God doesn't expect or intend for us to do it all ourselves. That's why He sent the Holy Spirit to us."

Claire was silent. "I do want to be a Christian," he said, "but I don't have any special feeling."

"What do you mean?" Chuck asked him. "What sort of feeling do you think you ought to have?"

"I don't know," Claire replied. "But I always thought a guy had to have a strange feeling or something of the sort."

The young Bible student paused.

"I guess that's one place where a lot of people have trouble," Chuck said. "Some people think that being saved is a mental process to determine not to sin anymore. Lots of people break with some sin in their lives but they're not saved. Salvation is repenting of your sin and by faith taking the Lord Jesus into your heart and life. You've got to admit before the Lord that you're a sinner and believe in your heart that He – God's Son – can take that sin away and give you eternal life."

"That sounds reasonable."

"Do you think you're ready to trust Christ as your Savior now?" Chuck asked persistently.

Claire nodded.

"Do you really mean that you're ready to step out as a Christian?" Chuck asked him. "That you're going to mean business with God from here on out? You know, it's a serious matter to take a stand for Christ. God will help you, but you've got to be willing to follow Him."

"I know that," Claire answered firmly. "I've gone over it a hundred times in my mind the last week or two."

"You're willing then to surrender everything to the Lord Jesus?" Chuck asked. "As far as you're concerned, every sin that the Holy Spirit points out in your life, with God's help, you're going to try to get rid of it?"

Claire nodded.

The three of them got down on their knees then, and Chuck directed the seeking boy in a halting prayer. Despite the fact that Claire had been in Sunday school and church regularly since before he could even walk, his prayer was stiff and stumbling. But it came from the depth of his heart.

They were still on their knees when the front door opened and Mr. and Mrs. Forester came in.

"Well," Mrs. Forester said, her voice rising sarcastically, "what's going on here? A prayer meeting?"

The three of them started at the sound of her voice and turned quickly.

"I–" Marilyn began.

And then Mrs. Forester recognized Claire Eaton. "Claire!" she cried. "What are you doing here?"

By this time Claire's face had gone ashen. He scrambled nervously to his feet. "I just had to talk to Chuck and Marilyn," he blurted. Then with a deep breath he said, "I'm a Christian now. I just trusted Jesus as my Savior!"

Mrs. Forester straightened. The color faded from her cheeks and her eyes widened.

"Marilyn!" she exclaimed under her breath. "How could you! *How could you!*"

CHAPTER 4

"I'VE GOT TO LIVE FOR CHRIST!"

Mrs. Forester was still standing in the doorway. She was staring in abject disbelief at her daughter, Chuck Martin, and Claire. Her face was white and drawn, and she had a hurt, defiant look in her eyes.

Almost involuntarily Marilyn moved closer to Chuck and took hold of his big hand, as though to draw strength from him. Harold Forester stood silently beside his wife. But now he stepped forward and shook Claire's hand.

"You've made a wonderful decision, son. I'm proud of you."

"I–I don't know how it's going to work out, sir," Claire answered doubtfully. "I don't know whether I'll be able to live the way I should or not."

"Of course you won't in your own strength," Marilyn's father went on. "God doesn't expect us to live the Christian life alone. All you've got to do is turn to Him for strength."

Claire shifted nervously from one foot to the other. "I don't even know for sure how a Christian is supposed to live," he said hesitantly. "I'll have to do a lot of serious thinking about a good many things."

"You're on the right track," Mr. Forester assured him. "Read your Bible and pray every day. Listen to Christian programs. When the Lord convinces you that there's something you ought to root out of your life, ask Him to help you tear it out by the roots!"

When Claire was gone and Marilyn and Chuck had gone down to the recreation room, Mrs. Forester turned to her husband.

"I hope you're satisfied, Harold Forester!" she snapped indignantly. "I've never been so humiliated in my life!"

He turned to face her. "I don't know what there is to humiliate anyone," he said. "A young man accepted Christ as Savior. We ought to be rejoicing."

Anger flickered in her eyes. For a moment she could not speak. When she did, her voice was low and tense. "Do you know who that was, Harold? Do you know who Marilyn and that–that Chuck person had down on his knees in our living room?"

Mr. Forester nodded. "That's all the more reason for rejoicing. Think what a testimony that boy can be! Think what an influence for the Lord he can be in school and what it would mean to his church if he could bring his parents to the Lord."

Mrs. Forester's lips were trembling. Small drops of perspiration beaded her forehead.

"What is Dr. Carpenter going to think?" she asked. "And what is Claire's father going to think?" She walked across the room and back again. "Harold," she said miserably, "what am I going to tell them when they come to me?"

He went to her, and taking her hand, drew her down on the couch beside him.

"You're looking at this thing all wrong, Carrie," he told her. "Any pastor and father ought to be happy to have a boy make a decision for Christ. And besides, the important thing isn't what Dr. Carpenter or Mr. Eaton think about it but that it actually happened. I think it's wonderful."

She pulled away from him, her lips stiffening to a firm, hard line. "You're so wrapped up in this fanatical religion business that you don't understand. You don't understand anything anymore. It–it's almost as though we're strangers. And we used to be so close."

She swallowed the lump in her throat and mopped at the tears that began to course down her cheeks.

"I haven't had a moment's happiness since you–since–." She didn't finish what she was saying. Instead, she got hurriedly to her feet and dashed upstairs.

Harold Forester stared after her. For a long while, long after Chuck had gone home and the others off to bed, he still remained on the couch, staring into the dying coals in the fireplace.

Then he got slowly to his knees and began to pray.

* * *

Claire Eaton went home that night, apprehensively. His dad was sitting in the library, poring over a brief. The books were piled high on the desk about him. He looked up as his son entered.

"You're home early, Claire," he said, pushing back the law book from which he had been studying. "The dance must have let out early."

Claire shook his head. "I didn't go."

"You didn't catch me missing any dances when I was your age," Mr. Eaton said. "Used to go to them all."

Claire still stood there, biting his lower lip nervously. "I–I went over to see Marilyn Forester and Chuck."

His dad went back to his law book.

"Dad," Claire broke in hoarsely, "I–I've got to talk to you."

"Certainly."

The boy crossed the room and sat down in a comfortable leather chair at one end of the desk.

"I–I wasn't going to tell you for a few days," Claire began, his voice breaking, "but I've just got to."

Mr. Eaton's forehead wrinkled. "What's the matter, Claire?" he asked. "Are you in some sort of trouble?"

He shook his head. "No, it isn't anything like that. The past two or three weeks I haven't been able to sleep or eat or study or do much of anything. I've been so upset I–."

"I'll make an appointment for you with Dr. Benton the first thing in the morning."

"But I don't need a doctor," Claire blurted. Sweat was standing out on his forehead and his hands were working nervously. "It's just that I–" he looked plaintively at his father.

Mr. Eaton sat back in his chair, eyeing his son critically.

"I don't know how to tell you, Dad, but I've become a Christian. I've confessed my sin and put my trust in the Lord Jesus."

The attorney drew in his breath sharply.

"What did you say?" he demanded.

"I'm a Christian now," the boy continued doggedly. "I've been fighting this thing for two or three weeks. That's why I haven't been able to sleep or eat. But it's all settled now."

"I can't understand you, Claire," his dad replied irritably. "You've been in Sunday school and church since you were in your mother's arms. What's all this nonsense about suddenly becoming a Christian? You've been a Christian all your life."

"That's where we've been mistaken, Dad," Claire protested. "I learned about Jesus during my years in Sunday school, but I never actually had given my heart to Him. I had never realized that I was a sinner and had to account for my sins. I had never been 'born again.'"

The handsome, gray-haired man straightened. With slow deliberation he picked up a pencil and began to turn it between his fingers.

"That's some of the stuff Marilyn Forester and her boyfriend have been pumping into you, isn't it?" he asked. His voice was soft enough but was edged with ice.

Claire did not answer. The silence in the library was electric. Mr. Eaton was staring into his son's eyes.

"I–I" Claire began, but the words choked off miserably.

"I knew something like this was going to happen and to think that it had to be my son. I told Dr. Carpenter when he first let those two lead youth group meetings. I warned him!" He pushed back from his chair and got noisily to his feet. "Now he'll have to answer to me!"

Claire Eaton went up to bed shortly after his father had stomped out of the library but try as he would, sleep would not come. Chuck and Marilyn and Mr. Forester had been so sure everything would work out. They had said that all he had to do was to read his Bible and pray. He choked convulsively. They just didn't know his dad.

The next morning when he got up and went downstairs to breakfast, his father had already gone.

"I suppose Dad told you about last night?" he said to his mother.

She nodded.

"I–I didn't want to make him angry," Claire went on. "I don't want to make anyone angry. But I've got to live for Christ, Mom! I've just got to!"

She sat down at the kitchen table across from him. She was a small woman with graying hair and kind eyes. "I don't know what this is all about, Claire," she said. "I don't understand it at all, but it seems it has done something to you. You seem different, a little older or grown up perhaps."

Groping hesitantly for words, he explained the way of salvation to his mother, telling of the load of sin he had felt and how he came to the place where he couldn't put the Lord off any longer. "I just couldn't go on alone any longer. I had to become a Christian!"

* * *

Claire Eaton was not the only one who had found sleep impossible that night. Mrs. Forester had been awake until the clock on the mantle struck five. The scene of what had happened in their living room a few hours before kept crowding her mind to torment her. She dozed at last, fitfully, until the alarm went off.

When breakfast was over, Marilyn went up to her. "Goodbye, Mom," she said, leaning over to kiss her. Mrs. Forester cooly turned her cheek.

She had known that Dr. Carpenter would come, but she hadn't expected him that morning. Still the instant the doorbell rang, only minutes after Harold and Marilyn and Kay had left, she knew who it was. Dr. Carpenter came striding into the living room, his eyes blazing.

"I–I know what you came to talk to me about," Mrs. Forester stammered. "I feel just as terrible about it as you do."

He stared coldly into her tear-reddened eyes.

"That is scarcely going to help, Mrs. Forester," he said. "It would be better for both of us if you could control yourself."

She bit her lower lip. "Won't you sit down?"

"What I have to say can be said standing," he retorted. "It was because of you that I permitted your daughter and this–this young upstart to take over the youth group. It was because you were so determined to have me work with them that I went against my better judgment and used them. This is the thanks I get!" His voice rose dramatically.

"I didn't know what was happening, Dr. Carpenter," she protested tearfully. "Honestly I didn't. I didn't know until we came home last night and found Claire here!"

"I had a phone call from the boy's father," the minister went on. His face was ashen, and his hands were clenched until the knuckles showed white. "This is serious, Mrs. Forester. A thing like this could cause me to lose my position!"

She started to cry, convulsively.

"I don't know what I've done," she wailed, "to be punished like this!"

CHAPTER 5

AN EARNEST STUDENT

The day after Claire gave his heart to the Lord, Chuck Martin chanced to meet him and Ron Orlis on the street.

"Hey, I'm glad to see you, Chuck," Claire said, his face lighting. "Have you got a few minutes? I'd like to talk to you."

"I'll be running along," Ron said. "Will we see you in Bible Club, Claire?"

"You sure will. I'll try to get a couple of my friends to go too."

When Ron was gone, Claire turned to Chuck. "I've got to talk to you."

"Sure thing. Why don't we go in here and have a dish of ice cream?"

"I had a terrible run-in with Dad last night," Claire confided when the waitress had taken their orders.

"Telling him about what I did last night was one of the hardest things I've ever done in my life."

"I'm glad you told him, Claire. There's something about giving your testimony to people to give strength that nothing else will."

"He blamed Dr. Carpenter," Claire went on. "I tried to tell him that nobody high-pressured me, that I had decided to give my heart to Jesus on my own, but he wouldn't listen."

"Don't worry about that, Claire. I'm glad you had backbone enough to speak up for the Lord."

The waitress brought the ice cream. Chuck shoved the check into his pocket.

"There's something else I've been wanting to talk to you about, Claire," the older boy said. "Now that you've made a decision for Christ, you're going to need a great deal of help to understand how He wants you to live and what you ought to leave out of your life."

Claire tapped the dish thoughtfully with the edge of his spoon. "But the trouble is, Chuck," he said, "I don't really know anything about the Bible. I've been going to Sunday school all the time, but we had lessons about being good to people and cleaning out the slums and all that sort of thing. I didn't even know until last night that the four Gospels told the same story."

"I know you're busy at school and all that," Chuck went on, "but do you suppose you and I could get together a couple of nights a week for Bible study?

We could go over some of these things and see what God's Word has to say about them."

They got together that evening at the home where Chuck Martin had a room. Together they went over the third chapter of John, emphasizing once more the need of spiritual rebirth.

"I know you became a Christian last night," Chuck said after he had finished reading the chapter aloud, "but I just wanted to call attention to these things, so you would have them firmly in mind. We can't be too careful about getting every one of these fundamentals just the way the Bible gives them."

They went on through the chapter, verse by verse, Claire asking the questions and Chuck answering them. At last they closed the Bible and began to pray.

"I–I'm afraid I'm not very good at this, Chuck," the new Christian said. "The only prayers I've ever said have been those I've learned and recited like poetry. I haven't had any practice praying."

Chuck looked up at him.

"You don't say prayers, Claire. You simply talk to God from your heart."

"I don't get it."

"Do you need practice to talk to your mom or dad or your girlfriend?" he asked.

Claire shook his head, grinning self-consciously.

"You want to remember that God is more interested in you than you are yourself," Chuck told him. "He wants you to come to Him with your problems.

He wants to help you live a consistent Christian life. But He isn't going to force Himself on you. You have to make the move. You have to be the one to come to Him, just as you came to Him to be saved."

Claire bit his lower lip thoughtfully. "I–I think I understand," he said.

* * *

Danny had been so busy with his work assignments in the church and his studies that he scarcely had an opportunity to talk with Chuck about Claire Eaton. He had heard only snatches of it as the story went about school. So he was highly interested when Kay stopped him in the hall.

"I've just got to tell you about Claire," she said, bubbling. "Marilyn was telling me this morning."

"That's wonderful," he said after she told him.

That evening Chuck Martin had just arrived at the Forester home, where he and Marilyn were going to study, when the telephone rang.

"I think I know who that is," Chuck said, getting to his feet and answering.

It was several minutes before he came back.

"Well, was it your other girl?" Marilyn asked, grinning.

He sat down without speaking. "Nope," he said. "The fact of the matter is that call concerned you as well as me." He paused for a moment.

"Was it about Claire?" she asked.

He nodded. Dr. Carpenter's secretary just called and said that he wanted to talk to me. It seems he'd been trying to get me all afternoon."

"He was over to see Mom this morning."

"That's what he informed me," the boy continued. "He said that he will no longer need our services at First Church. He is going to take over the work of the youth group personally until he can undo the harm that has been done."

"Oh, Chuck! Does he really feel that way?"

He also informed me that he and Mr. Eaton insist that you and I leave Claire alone. He says we have the poor boy so confused that he scarcely knows what he is doing or saying.

CHAPTER 6

WINNING OUT

There were services at First Church that evening, but Mrs. Forester refused to go.

"I'll never set foot inside that church again, Harold," she informed her husband angrily. "You should have heard the way Dr. Carpenter talked to me. Why, I've never been so humiliated in my life."

Harold Forester looked up from his book. "Why?" he asked. "What's happened now?"

She walked over to the kitchen table and sat down across from him. Her lower lip was trembling uncertainly, and the powder on her face was streaked. "You know what's wrong, Harold!" she snapped. "But I can't really blame Dr. Carpenter after what happened or John Eaton either." Her face clouded. "To think that my own daughter would do such a thing to me! I'll never get over it!"

Harold Forester set down his book.

"Now just a minute, Carrie," he said. "Marilyn hasn't done anything of which she should be ashamed. She and Chuck talked with Claire Eaton about his soul. I've done the same thing with his father. The only difference is that Claire saw his need of a Savior."

Mrs. Forester got slowly to her feet. For a moment or two she grasped the back of her chair for support and stared down at him with brimming eyes.

"Harold," she said when she could trust her voice, "you know what an outstanding church leader John Eaton has been. He has taught in the Sunday school and has filled in when the minister has been ill. Why, he has even represented us at the State conventions. And you've talked with him as though he were a common ordinary sinner." She sat down again, nervously, pushing at her hair with trembling fingers. "I'll never be able to face John Eaton again."

Harold Forester did not answer his wife immediately. He closed his book and laid it aside.

"Carrie," he said at last, "you're getting all worked up over nothing. I haven't hurt my relationship with John Eaton, nor yours either. We've been business friends for years, and there's no reason why we won't go on being good friends. But I have talked, very seriously, with him about his soul. And," he took a deep breath, "if I get another opportunity, I intend to talk with him again."

Mrs. Forester swallowed hard. "I can understand now why I only get defiance from Marilyn," she groaned. "She's taught it right here at home."

And then, before her husband had an opportunity to answer her, she turned and fled to her room upstairs.

* * *

Attorney John Eaton was coldly indifferent when his son told him that he would like to attend the little church where Marilyn and Chuck and the other kids went.

"You haven't considered my wishes in any of this, Claire," his dad said. "I don't imagine it would make much difference what I want you to do. You'd probably do as you please anyway."

"It isn't that I want to do something that you don't want me to, Dad," Claire stammered, fumbling for words. "But I would like to go to the same church where Chuck goes. And I'd like to be with the other kids too."

"We have a fine, sensible religion at First Church," the lawyer said evenly, "and the young people of the town's finest people go there. You will have to think of a better reason than that."

The boy stood there, miserably, without speaking. John Eaton waited.

"You're on an emotional binge right now, Claire," he said at last. "You've stumbled onto this narrow, bigoted religion and it sounds wonderful to you. You're going to convert the world. But you'll get over it soon enough. Once the shine wears off, you'll find that it isn't as glorious as you seem to think it is." He turned back to his magazine. "Go to any church you like, but when you come to your senses, I think Dr. Carpenter will be gracious enough to take you back."

Claire told Chuck and Marilyn about his conversation with his father that evening after youth group.

"I'm glad your dad gave you permission to come over here to church," Chuck answered. "However, a person ought to obey his parents, in the Lord."

Claire nodded.

"I had already made up my mind that if Dad said I had to go to First Church that was what I was going to do."

They walked out onto the street.

"But it wouldn't have changed me," Claire went on.

Claire attended every meeting that he could. He listened attentively, and in the discussions at youth group and Sunday school, he asked questions at every opportunity.

"I don't believe I've ever seen anyone as interested in the things of the Lord as he is," Marilyn said to Chuck one evening after church when Claire pushed past them suddenly and rushed outside. "Did you see that look on his face just now? He was deeply moved."

Chuck nodded.

Although Claire's salvation was the talk of the school, no one was as excited about it as Roxie Orlis.

"Just think, Danny," she said excitedly when she first heard the news, "Claire's the star on the basketball team and editor of the school paper and – just about the most popular guy in school."

"What's the matter, Roxie?" Ron grinned. "Got a crush on him?"

"Of course not," she retorted frigidly. "I was just thinking how wonderful it is going to be as far as his testimony is concerned. You ought to hear the girls at school talk about him. Why, they think he's something out of this world."

"It does mean a lot when a guy like that follows the Lord," Danny acknowledged. "As far as the Lord is concerned though this guy isn't any different than anyone else. But when it comes to the world, it seems to make a lot of difference who the person is and what he can do. Somehow they get the idea that being a Christian is only for those who are weak and so low in intelligence that they aren't able to do much of anything. When they see someone who does have a lot on the ball and who follows the Lord Jesus, they are surprised and pay a lot of attention to him."

"Claire's going to come to Bible Club too," Roxie continued. "I talked with three or four of the girls this afternoon, and they had already heard about it. They said that if Claire would be there, they might come too."

Her twin brother grinned. "That's great," he told her. "It's sure amazing the way God can change a person's heart when He gets hold of him, isn't it?"

THE
DANNY ORLIS
SERIES

The Danny Orlis series, by Bernard Palmer, delivers a blend of adventure, mystery, and suspense through various settings—from the Canadian wilderness to Guatemalan jungles. Danny Orlis, an adept outdoorsman, skilled athlete, and committed Christian, employs his quick thinking, calm bravery, and biblical solutions to confront everyday problems and hair-raising dangers. Early stories focus on Danny navigating school life, sports, and outdoor challenges, while in later books, Danny and his wife Kay provide wisdom and guidance to youngsters facing lifelike situations and challenges. Having sold over two million copies, this series has made Palmer a renowned author in Christian youth literature. Palmer is also the author of the Felicia Cartright series and various other series for Christian youth.

AVAILABLE FROM WWW.ANEKOPRESS.COM